THE RELUCTANT ADVENTURES

OF

FLETCHER CONNOLLY

ON THE

INTERSTELLAR RAILROAD

VOLUME 2

INTERGALACTIC BOGTROTTER

F. R. SAVAGE

THE RELUCTANT ADVENTURES OF FLETCHER
CONNOLLY ON THE INTERSTELLAR RAILROAD
VOLUME 2
INTERGALACTIC BOGTROTTER

First published in the United States of America in 2016 by Knights Hill Publishing.

Cover art by Christian Bentulan
Interior design and layout by Felix R. Savage

ISBN-10:1-937396-21-5
ISBN-13:978-1-937396-21-3

THE RELUCTANT ADVENTURES

OF

FLETCHER CONNOLLY

ON THE

INTERSTELLAR RAILROAD

VOLUME 2

INTERGALACTIC BOGTROTTER

CHAPTER 1

Going by the looks of her you'd assume the *Hellraiser* deserves her name. She's a decommissioned Lockheed-Martin F-99, a quarter of a mile long, shaped like a manta ray, barnacled with railguns and energy weapons. But she handles like a swine, and I should know—I've piloted her most of the way back to Arcadia, while Kenneth, who's supposed to be doing it, humps Vanessa in the ammo locker. Vanessa is our sole surviving propulsion technician. The Captain's asked her to do something about the gurgling noise you can hear on the engineering deck, but she says it's just the plumbing.

I am slumped in the pilot's couch when the Captain charges onto the bridge, his brow furrowed. "Have you seen my iPhone?"

"No, I haven't. What do you need it for?"

It's not as if we can get a signal on the Interstellar Railroad.

The Captain rummages in the lockers and drawers where the *Hellraiser's* former owners kept their stuff. "Iphone,

iPhone!" he says. It's the 2063 model he's got. It's supposed to sing out when you shout for it. Out of various crannies drift obscene greetings from phones belonging to dead pirates. The Captain chucks them into the e-waste bin.

"Why do you need your phone?" says Harriet, our life-support officer. She's huddled at the navigation table, nursing a treecat and a cup of tea.

"It's got the bloody insurance documents on it!" the Captain says. "The pictures and everything."

He is referring to the final pictures he took of our doomed ship, the *Skint Idjit*. She was eaten three weeks ago by A-tech artefacts that looked like giant butterflies. Half our crew were eaten, too.

We had to blow up the poor old *Idjit,* with the dead inside her, and decamp to the *Hellraiser,* whose entire crew had already been eaten, except for Kenneth and his boss, whose death no one regrets. We are now eleven, down from 28. It may seem heartless for the Captain to be obsessing over the insurance documents, but he's coping better than Harriet, who is too traumatized to do anything except cry into her tea. She thinks we will be going home soon. Poor Harriet.

I heard her ask the Captain this morning: "Are you totally against living in New Jersey?" And him, the coward: "I've not really made up my mind …" Cue nagging, sobbing, and the Captain stomping off the bridge in a huff.

As for me, I'm getting out of this life. I've had enough. I'm going to find myself an uninhabited planet in the Perseus arm. I've made up my mind. I just haven't worked out how to tell the Captain yet.

I slide lower into the pilot's couch. On the viewscreen in front of me, the Interstellar Railroad races away under the

Hellraiser's nose at three lightyears per hour. It looks like a ghostly ladder stretching into the utter blackness of folded space. When you're sitting here for hours, your eyes play tricks on you—is it stretching up, or down, or straight ahead? The answer is none of the above, because the Railroad is beyond human comprehension. Scientists think it connects all the habitable planets in the Milky Way, but that's really just a guess. We've been using it for forty years, and we still haven't a clue where it came from or how it works. We don't even know where it *goes,* mostly.

"Look what I found," the Captain says. He makes a sound I hardly recognize, I've not heard it in so long. He's laughing. Holding up an iPad. *"Feck Off With You: Butterfly-Zilla, An Epic Poem.* Fletch, did you write this?"

"Guilty," I say.

It's my version of crying into my tea.

"Listen!" the Captain declaims,

> We of the *Skint Idjit,* in the year of 2066,
> hearing that others had found A-tech treasures
> through dumb luck, journeyed forth with high hopes
> along the unexplored Beta Aurigae Spur.
> Often our Captain, Donal the Dimwit,
> gave orders to the crew which we ignored,
> saying, "Feck off with you. We shall get rich
> whether or not we play blackjack on the bridge
> and eat raw cookie dough out of the freezer."
> He then sought recompense for that …

"Did you really write that, Fletch?" Harriet says.

"It's brilliant!" Donal says, chortling as he skims the rest of the poem.

"Someone's read *Beowulf,*" says Gordon from his corner.

"I was just bored," I say.

"No, but this is brilliant." Donal laughs out loud and starts quoting the bit where I tried to disguise the Butterfly-zillas as the bodies of our lost scouts—*not* my finest hour.

With relief I spot something new on the viewscreen. In the distance, the Railroad widens and splits into a tangled cloverleaf arrangement.

"We're here!" I shout to Gordon. He raises a hand in acknowledgement. "Everyone strap in!"

I steer into the junction, narrowly missing a Boeing X-700. The Arcadia junction is one of the most heavily trafficked in the galaxy. It's only two stops from Earth, and spurs of the Railroad fork off from here to every bleeding place. I shoot the Boeing a noseful of graywater from the *Hellraiser's* toilets, which is the Interstellar Railroad equivalent of a middle finger. My spirits are lifting already.

Through the junction, we zoom onto the local loop, the section of the Railroad that encircles Arcadia. At a nod from Gordon, I hurl the *Hellraiser* off into orbital space. There's a violent jolt before the inertial dampeners kick in. Harriet's tea mug flies off the arm of her couch, and the treecats yowl.

A solid layer of yellow-gray cloud wraps Arcadia, as always. We tear through the clouds and glide down to the surface, which is bare rock, scoured by some long-forgotten alien war. The spaceport is the place where all the spaceships are standing around, colorful dots on the granite plain.

"Nice flying," says Gordon to me when we've safely landed.

"I'm especially proud of my hand signals," I say, giving as good as I get.

Gordon F. Poole, to give him his full appellation, is our stacker—the guy who operates the ship. He's seventy-eight, dapper, and sarcastic. We borrowed him from my uncle Finian after the loss of the *Skint Idjit*. I don't actually dislike him, it's his music I can't stand. I have had 20th-century rock 'n' roll droning in my ears for the last three weeks.

It's blissfully quiet down here, despite the rumble of spaceships taking off and landing in the distance. Gordon and I are standing under the *Hellraiser's* nose, wearing rain ponchos and breathing masks because the air on Arcadia is shite. Acid rain drips off the cowling of the sensor blisters overhead. The Captain prowls around, inspecting the landing gear and the chain dogs. Harriet watches miserably from the airlock steps.

"I'm just going into Tretyakovsky," I shout to the Captain. "Is there anything we need?"

He hurries over and launches into a shopping list. It starts with black paint and ends with, "Ah, never mind, I'll go in myself. Just pick up some lager and crisps! We'll catch up on the footie. I've downloaded last week's Galway United match, it looks like a grand game."

Now I feel like shite.

"Going to see Finian, are you?" Gordon says when the Captain is out of earshot.

How did he guess? His IQ starts with a 2, that's how.

"Yeah, I thought I'd drop by if I can track him down. You coming?"

5

"I think I'll stay and advise Donal. He may need it if he's going to DON'T TOUCH THAT!"

Gordon can move quite fast for a gent of his years.

I trudge off into the drizzle. It's a long walk to the nearest terminal—independents always get the worst parking spaces. Half an hour later, my throat is itching and I've got a coronet of burns on my forehead where the rain always gets in around your mask. I squelch into the terminal and plod down a long, long flight of alien stairs.

Arcadia is riddled with underground bunkers, formerly Aladdin's caves of A-tech. That was forty years ago. Now the A-tech has all been claimed, patented, and reverse-engineered, and the bunkers are home to hundreds of thousands of people who mostly work in the tech and services sectors. I met a woman here last year who'd come out to work for Samsung, and ended up driving a space taxi for the mob. That's the kind of place this is. *And* they've put the prices of the rent-a-bikes up again. Bloody Russians! They'd charge for breathing if they thought they could get away with it.

By the time I reach Finian's hotel, I am in a vile mood, not improved by the discovery that he's staying at the Four Seasons on Reservoir Square. The security guards grab me as I'm about to get on the elevator. I glimpse myself in the mirrors. Dirty Wranglers, dirtier blond hair, those awful acid-burns on my forehead, my expression ugly as I give out to the security guards—I do not look like the sort of person who stays here, indeed.

But neither does Finian and yet here he is, lounging in an alien-built penthouse with twenty-foot ceilings and the telly on full blast. Him and his mates, the crew of the *Marauding*

Elephant, have spread out across the entire top floor of the hotel. They greet me with cheerful cries of "How's she cuttin', Fletch?" They're eating fancy takeaways and swearing at the big screen where Cork City is trouncing Galway United. This must be the same game Donal downloaded. It looks better here than it ever would in the gloomy mess of the *Hellraiser.* And there are fresh flowers everywhere, and the floor-to-ceiling windows look out over Reservoir Square, where tourists are splashing in the bunker's de-acidified water supply. My uncle's had his beard braided, with wee gold elephants on the ends.

I was going to buy my own planet. It wouldn't have to be a luxury world. I'd settle for a fixer-upper.

Maybe I'll have enough left for a second-hand world after I split the money with Donal.

"I take it Goldman Sachs paid out," I say.

"Seven hundred million dollars," Finian says, watching my face.

I pretend to be unimpressed. "You should have held out for ten figures."

"They were keen enough," he says, with his boots up on the sofa, sipping a pint. "So keen they came out from Earth themselves to get the A-tech. In a bleeding Pentagon spaceship with anti-matter particle cannons. When the CFO of an investment bank offers you a choice between a check and a hole in your hull, you take the check. That's a pro tip, lad." His laugh turns into a belch. "Want a pint?"

"Sure."

The A-tech artefacts Finian is referring to are the ones that destroyed the *Skint Idjit.* I called them Butterfly-zillas. They looked like Cthulhu in drag, and acted like it too.

7

They'd vampire the energy out of *anything*, be it human beings, ships, or planets. I'm sure you can see the military applications.

Finian should have held out for *eleven* figures.

Still, $700 million is not a small sum and, as previously agreed, 40% of it will soon be mine. I was going to keep it all for myself, but I can't do that to the Captain. He's my oldest friend. We grew up together in Lisdoonvarna. So I'll give him half the money—that'll be $140 million—and he can do whatever he likes with it. I know Harriet wants him to retire from the exploration business. Then I'll take my half and see what I can get for it in the Perseus arm.

There's a wet bar in an alcove off the suite. Waitresses wobble to and fro on stiletto heels matching their Playboy Bunny outfits. One of them brings me a pint on a silver tray, and I nearly drop it.

The 'waitress' is Jacob Ruby with fake titties, lipstick, and fishnets on his hairy legs.

My uncle pisses himself laughing. "Did youse see his face? Fecking hell, that was priceless."

"Discovered your inner service worker, Ruby?" I say.

Jacob Ruby was my assistant on the *Skint Idjit*. Goldman Sachs, who funded our expedition on the Beta Aurigae spur, planted him on us to protect their investment. He's a stacker. I handed him over to Finian at the same time as I gave my uncle a bag full of Butterfly-zillas to sell for me.

The deal was that Ruby would make sure GS coughed up a fair price for the Butterfly-zillas. It obviously worked, so I'm surprised Ruby hasn't gone running back to his cubicle. He must have liked it on the *Marauding Elephant,* after all.

"I'm transitioning," he says with dignity.

Jesus, was it *that* bad?

"I thought he deserved his share," Finian says, watching Ruby's fake buttocks wiggle away. For a second I wonder if my uncle is riding that. The image is so horrible I reject it immediately, but I'm sure the force of Finian's personality is to blame in some way for Ruby's strange—*and expensive*—decision.

"Just as long as his share's not coming out of my share," I say.

Finian meets my eyes steadily. "I'm not giving you any of the money, Fletch."

I knew it, *I knew it.* This is why I've been in such a shite mood. Some part of my brain *knew* he was going to stiff me out of my share.

"Got any particular reason for being a lying, cheating gobshite today? Or is this just another day in Finian-land?" I manage to keep my voice from shaking.

"You'll not talk to me that way." His blue eyes go paler, like quartz. "You can be a man about it or the lads can throw you out. Your choice."

"We had an agreement."

"I promised to give you forty percent. *And I did.*"

He gestures to my belt, where my hand has come to rest on the hilt of my lightsaber. This is not some toy out of a Star Wars movie. It's a genuine A-tech weapon. I picked it up on the Draco spur twenty years ago, when I was working for Finian.

"I gave you that, didn't I?" he says.

"Did you feck. I stole it off you." Hearing these words come out of my mouth, I wince. I've been denying I stole it off him for decades and now he's tricked me into admitting it.

"You stole it off me," he repeats, amusement creeping into his eyes, "and I let you keep it."

He swings his boots off the sofa and reaches one huge wrinkly hand inside his denim jacket. His own lightsaber pops into his hand. With the beam switched off, it looks like a ten-inch baton, decorated with swirly alien runes. A detachable powerpack swings down like a stock. It's the twin of mine.

"This," says Finian, "is worth at least two-fifty mil. There are only six of them in the universe and I personally know fellas who'd pay more than that to have one of their own. So if you want ready cash, you can sell yours. I'll put you onto a buyer."

I look around at the auld fellas. They are earwigging like mad. I decide not to provide them with any more free entertainment. "Thanks for the tip, Uncle, I'll let you know if I'm interested." I set down my half-drunk pint and start for the door.

"Did Donal come back with you?" Finian calls after me.

"He did."

"Tell him to give me a bell if he wants someone to take that old F-99 off his hands."

"Are you buying ships now?"

He guffaws. "Of course I am. What else do you think an old pirate like me would spend three-quarters of a billion dollars on? I'm equipping a whole, ahem, *exploration* fleet. Connolly's Marauders," he brags.

CHAPTER 2

The *Hellraiser's* lights guide me back through the pitch blackness of an Arcadian night. My mind is filled with fantasies of grinding my fist into Finian's face. I am not a violent man. My preferred method of dealing with danger is to pop into the jacks and wait until it's gone. But this is something different.

I would prefer a cunning and subtle revenge, all else being equal. But all else *isn't* equal. He's got $700 million and I haven't.

The yellow LEDs on the *Hellraiser's* undercarriage shine down on anti-grav gliders heaped with DIY supplies. Donal must have bought that lot on credit. I happen to know he's got exactly twice as much ready cash as I do: $127. All his capital was tied up in the *Skint Idjit*.

He's standing by the stairs, talking to a couple of fellas in full-body breathing masks. I am about to slide past them without a word when the smell of clove vapor alerts me to Gordon's presence.

The old stacker pulls me into the shadows behind the landing gear. "Those men are from Goldman Sachs."

"Bollocks."

But now I see they're talking *at* Donal, not to him. He just stands there nodding and shaking his head.

"They want him to refund their investment in the *Skint Idjit.*"

"They can't do that, can they?"

"I used to work for Barclays, Fletch. Believe me: they can."

"Well, they can whistle for it. The *Idjit's* gone. They can take a trip out the Beta Aurigae spur and see for themselves."

"That's the point. The ship's gone; so are their chances of getting a return on their investment."

"Then they can wait for the insurance to pay out."

"The insurance isn't going to pay out."

"Oh, bloody … It's a con game, isn't it? The system's rigged. They're all in it together to squeeze the little guys dry. Blood from a fecking stone in our case. Good luck to them."

"That's your near-total ignorance of finance speaking," Gordon says crisply. "I am not defending the morality of the system. I'm just telling it like it is. Donal owes those gentlemen fifty million dollars, yesterday." The LED of his e-cig glows behind his breathing mask. He's got this gizmo which holds the e-cig near his mouth, so he can vape without taking his mask off. I can smell it even through my own mask. "But that's all right, isn't it?" he says. "You'll be able to advance him the requisite sum."

"What're you talking about?"

"Those hideous A-tech weapons. I know you gave them to Finian, and you'd hardly have done that without expectation of reward." Gordon laughs dryly.

I don't deny it. I don't have to. "He's given me feck all reward."

"Are you serious?"

"Serious as a heart attack."

I go and fetch the other lads out of the ship. The Goldman Sachs reps beat a retreat shortly after that. With wankers like those, you've not got to even clear your throat in their direction. Loitering at them will do the trick. But they've still got all the power, including the power to bankrupt us. I personally wouldn't notice the difference. It's our other backers who'd feel it. Our families and friends, who took a punt on the *Skint Idjit* and have already lost that, but it could get worse …

"My dad persuaded half of County Clare to invest in us," Donal moans, head in his hands. "The bastards'll take their cars, their houses …"

"My parents could lose their house," cries Harriet.

I stay silent. My family did not invest a penny in the *Idjit*. My dad explained at the time that he was damned if he'd pay for me to follow in Finian's footsteps.

Kenneth, sole survivor of the *Hellraiser's* original crew, has nothing at stake. But Vanessa has an apartment in Seattle that she doesn't want to lose, and the South Africans all have kids in private school or extended polygamous families of three hundred to support, or some bloody thing, I don't know, Jesus, I don't *know* how people get themselves so entangled with others.

"We'll just have to sell the *Hellraiser*," Harriet says with finality.

That's her mistake. That tone of finality. And the hint of a smile. It reminds us that this is what she has wanted all along.

"No," Donal says.

He stands up. Puts on his breathing mask. Then his poncho.

We all watch him leave the bridge. He walks with such a heavy tread it sounds like he's still wearing that exoskeleton, the one he nearly got killed in.

Harriet sobs. The others all look at me expectantly.

I grind my teeth and go after him.

"Donal! *Donal!* Where are you, you idjit?"

Back outside. It's a still, perfectly black night. Thanks to Arcadia's permanent cloud cover, there are no stars, only the pilot lights of other spaceships in the distance. At least it's not raining anymore.

"Donal!"

"Up here."

I follow his voice to the nose of the ship, and bark my shin on one of the anti-grav gliders. Supplies roll hither and yon. I scramble after bug repellent, rolls of duct tape, air fresheners, a twelvepack of inspirational posters— "Donal, you bought inspirational posters? That's a waste of money. You should have just bought a violin."

He used to play the fiddle. Fecking gifted he is too. We'd have some grand ceilis when he was in the mood, with Shaka joining in on the buckets. But his fiddle got smashed in the mud of Suckass.

"Violins are expensive," he says from somewhere up in the air. "Inspirational posters are cheap."

"Yeah, that's my point." I move out from under the nose of the ship, and crane my head back. High above, his headlamp glints over the edge of one of the anti-grav gliders. "What the feck are you doing?"

The glider descends. It's just a flat platform with an anti-grav engine underneath and a handle at the back. Donal's standing in the middle. "Come here a minute."

I step on, and smell paint. The glider rises back up to the nose of the *Hellraiser*.

But she is no longer the *Hellraiser*. Donal has painted a new name on her, in sloppy glow-in-the-dark blue letters. The paint runs into the pocks in her steel nose shield.

I read her new name, and sigh.

"What do you think?" Donal says.

"People used to ask me where the *Skint Idjit* got her name from. I'd tell them that's no mystery. The Captain named her after himself."

"Yeah, I've heard that before. So this time I decided to name her after you."

The ship's new name is: *Intergalactic Bogtrotter*.

"That's brutal, Donal. I'm never going to live that down."

"I was thinking about *Muck Savage,* so consider yourself lucky."

"I'm not objecting to 'bogtrotter.' It's *intergalactic*. Inter means *between,* so it should be in*tra*galactic. The Railroad doesn't go to the bloody Andromeda Galaxy."

"That we're aware of."

"Jesus, I hope not. The problem is now everyone in *this* galaxy will think either you don't know English, or you can't spell."

He is silent for a minute. "Well, it'll hardly be the first time the rest of you have had to pay for my mistakes," he says quietly.

That is when I know I'm staying. I suppose I knew it all

along, really.

"Feck off," I say, giving him a punch. *"You* can tell Harriet and the rest we're not selling."

I'll just stick around until he's back on his feet. It won't be forever. There'll still be planets on the market when … when we've made $50 million, and then another few hundred million on top of that … oh Jesus, I've never been in a hole this deep.

"There'll be jobs to pick up," Donal says. "Even if it's just cargo runs. We'll pay off the bloodsuckers, and then we'll start saving for a new exploration trip. One big A-tech find, and our worries will be over!"

He even manages to convince the others that this is a possibility. When Donal is on form, he could talk a slug into a salt-shaker. But faces lengthen again over the next few days as jobs are not to be found. Gordon discovers that Goldman Sachs has put the word out—we are *their* prey and no one else's. Even the big tech companies are scared of the investment banks. They won't hire us for so much as a cargo run, and meanwhile Donal and Harriet max out their credit cards paying for repairs, and we still owe the bloodsuckers $50 million *plus interest*.

The South Africans start openly checking the want ads.

And I do what I knew all along I'd have to do.

I go back to the Four Seasons.

Finian's hosting a mob wives' kaffeeklatch this morning, at least that's the impression I get from all the fur and black-lace cleavage bouncing around.

"Are you still adding ships to your fleet?"

CHAPTER 3

"Sit down, Fletch," Finian says. "How are things?"

I hitch my arse on the foot of the circular bed where Finian's sprawling in rock-star style, shirt open, medallions glittering in his white chest fur. On the other side of the bed, several women are using Ruby as a jewellery model. He smiles and poses as they drape him with trinkets.

"Regarding the fleet," Finian says. "I'm at full strength at this point."

"Ah. Gotcha."

I'm gathering myself to leave when he adds, "But we still need a supply ship."

The auld sadist.

"Would this be a partnership?" I say. Finian knows we've got no funds to kick in. "Or a work for hire sort of thing?"

"Work for hire," he says. "No profit-sharing, but I'd be willing to offer a 10% completion bonus."

For sheer capitalistic ruthlessness, there's no investment banker can touch a pirate.

"In that case, we're in," I say. I don't need to confirm with Donal. We have no other options.

We hash out the details. My attention wanders. I keep looking at the women.

"Is it true what I hear he's called that ship?" Finian says. *"Intergalactic Bogtrotter?"*

"It's memorable, isn't it?"

"Yeah, but it's spelled wrong. Unless he's found a spur of the Railroad going to the Andromeda Galaxy ..." Finian chortles.

I slide off the bed and edge around the groups of chattering women.

"I need to know your cargo capacity to the inch," Finian yells after me. "I've got a powerful lot of supplies to pack in there."

I nod and lift a hand in farewell. I am focused on one of the woman, who is high-stepping ahead of me, towing an anti-grav suitcase.

I catch up with her outside the elevator. "Hello, Imogen, long time no see."

She frowns at me blankly.

"The Pravda? My friend was incapacitated? You gave us a lift into orbit?"

"Oh my God," says Imogen Kincaid. A expression of mild panic tightens her features. She stabs the elevator button in a vain attempt to get away quicker.

When I met Imogen last year, she was driving a space taxi for the Bratva—the hard men who run Arcadia. It's not really accurate to call them the mob. They mostly work as enforcers for the tech companies.

Imogen double-crossed me, trying to retrieve a certain item the Bratva were after. I had the last laugh, however. The last I saw of her, she was hot-rodding it away from the

Skint Idjit, with two Bratva pathetically tumbling after her on re-entry parachutes.

Now she's making an early exit from one of Finian's networking parties and it can't be because of me; she clearly didn't recognize me at all until I said hello. It's nice to know I've the kind of face that women remember.

Then again, I almost didn't recognize her, either. The cute geek-girl bob has turned into a trendy geometrical cut, the unisex smock has been replaced by a mob-wife ensemble of minidress and fur jacket, and she's wearing make-up. High heels bring her stature almost up to my shoulder.

She nearly falls over on the heels, hurrying into the elevator. I catch her. "Steady. What's in the suitcase?"

It is almost too big to fit into the elevator.

"It's a *safe,*" she says witheringly.

The floor indicator lights tick down. I can smell her perfume.

"So the last time we met, you were driving a space taxi." I'm desperately trying to think how to not let her get away. "You were an ace pilot. Really the best I've seen." It may sound like I'm buttering her up, but she flew that taxi with fearlessness *and* precision, a rare combination. Anyway she's much better than me. I hate piloting. "Are you not doing that anymore?"

She pivots to face me. "You completely fucked that up for me, OK? I got scapegoated for the whole thing. It was like 'Don't let the door hit you on the way out.' You would not *believe* how many people are waiting in line for jobs as *taxi drivers.*"

Actually, I would believe it, having spent the last few days covertly checking the want ads myself. I got as far as filling in an application for a scout job before resigning myself to my fate.

"Still, it doesn't look like you're hurting," I say.

We squeeze out into the mirrored foyer. She wraps the strap of her safe around her wrist, and does that sigh-snort thing only American women can manage. And Canadian ones. She's Canadian, mustn't forget that. They don't like being mistaken for Americans. *"Uccccch.* I'm selling bling to rich bitches who are so buuusy, they can't even make time to go shopping." She puts on a shrill voice. "'Oh, that's *adorable* on you!' Like, *not,* you heifer. Seriously, I'm prostituting my *soul* here." We pass out into Reservoir Square. "But the commission is OK."

Imogen stops on the sidewalk, scanning the traffic.

"Sounds like a gas," I say. "Who's supplying the product?"

A lumpy lad, sat sideways on a Ducatti at the corner, looks up from his iPhone and waves. He is wearing sunglasses and a Lokomotiv Moscow hoodie.

"Meet the new boss, same as the old boss," Imogen says bleakly. "There's no one else *to* work for on this planet."

Hoodie Man gets off his bike and lumbers towards us.

"Oh yes, there is," I say. "You just met him."

"Huh?"

"Do you even know whose hotel suite you were just in?"

"Oh, the old dude? You know who he reminded me of? Have you ever seen *The King of Wolf 1061c?* It's like that actor got old and fat and grew a beard." She giggles. "Totally fucking cool. He bought some of my stuff."

Hoodie Man is nearly on top of us.

"He's organizing a big expedition," I say urgently. "Are you interested?"

"Oh, an exploration trip?" She wrinkles her nose. "I'm really not the thrills and spills type."

"No thrills, hopefully no spills, just tagging along behind with the supplies. There's a 10% completion bonus."

Hoodie Man glares at me from behind his sunglasses. He snaps his fingers for Imogen to surrender the safe.

"Hmm," she says. "Where to?"

CHAPTER 4

"Omega Centauri," says Donal. "Omega fecking Centauri!"

He has just come back from his meeting with Finian. We are prepping the *Intergalactic Bogtrotter* for launch. This is like doing a thousand-piece jigsaw in three dimensions. It's ridiculous the amount of stuff Finian wants us to take.

And now we know why.

"Omega Centauri is four point one kiloparsecs from here," Donal says. *"Twice* as far as we went up the Beta Aurigae Spur!" He cackles at the thought. The stars are back in his eyes, and I suppose I should be pleased, but dark premonitions clamor at the back of my mind. There's only one reason for going that far out on the Railroad, bypassing any number of unexplored spurs closer to Earth, and that is to make mischief.

"Who's this?" Donal says, focusing on the poncho-clad figure at my side.

"Ah yes," I grin. "Meet Imogen Kincaid, our new pilot."

"Nice to meet you," Donal says doubtfully.

We climb the stairs. From the 40-foot height of the airlock, I spy a flock of water tankers driving our way to pump their contents into the *Bogtrotter's* tanks. Why is Finian wanting us to take so much water? It's a given in the exploration business that water is one thing you *don't* need to take much of. The Railroad only goes to habitable planets. Habitable planets, by definition, have water. When you run low, you stop and fill up. If you're a halfway-thorough explorer, you're stopping at every planet anyway. What's the old devil got in mind?

On the other side of the airlock, we remove our masks and outerwear. Donal takes in Imogen's crooked smile, her pretty brown eyes, and as much as can be seen of her curvaceous figure given that she's gone back to her own fashion tastes. Today it's a shapeless pinafore thing with striped fleece leggings. Donal smiles and shakes her hand. "Welcome aboard."

Harriet drags her away for the guided tour. "Is that your only bag? It looks like a safe, what've you got in there?"

As soon as they are out of earshot, Donal pulls his hair. "I'm happy for you, Fletch, I really am. But would she not settle for a different job? How about treecat wrangler? We need one of those."

I consider correcting his assumption that Imogen is my girlfriend, and decide to leave it. "Pilot it is, Donal. She's good. You wait till you see her sub-orbital moves."

"But we've already got a pilot! What's Kenneth going to say?"

We arrive on the bridge and there is Kenneth himself, in his mohawked and metallic-tattooed glory, eating instant ramen and watching the 2066 Eurovision finals on the navigation screen. "Ukraine's going to walk off with it," he greets us.

"Kenneth," I say, "is not a pilot."

"Huh? I am!"

"Yeah, and I'm the CEO of Goldman Sachs," I say. "We've only your word for it. When we captured this ship, everyone else was dead."

Actually, it was Finian and his Old Elephants who captured the ship, but the point stands.

"There was only you left alive, cowering on the bridge. You *said* you were the pilot, but where's the proof? You've certainly not been in a hurry to demonstrate your skills. *I* flew this pig of a ship all the way here because you were conveniently never to be found when wanted."

The loo flushes and Vanessa comes out. She plops herself defiantly on Kenneth's lap. "OK, fine," she says. "No, he wasn't the pilot. Shut up, Ken. He was the cook. But there's nothing wrong with that! Anyway, if you try and kick him off now, I'm going with him."

Still stinging about the way I had to fill in for him, I'm about to call her bluff when Donal turns the situation around. "You were the cook? That's fantastic! We lost our old cook back on the Beta Aurigae Spur." Poor Trigger. He'll never break another microwave. "Consider yourself reassigned, Ken. It's a much more important job," he winks.

I'm still skeptical. I've never yet met a cook who would willingly eat instant ramen.

Imogen comes onto the bridge with Harriet. "Did I miss something?"

"Nothing at all," I sigh.

"Fletch, why didn't you tell me about these little guys?!" Imogen has got a treecat on her shoulder. Harriet is also carrying her favorite, a tabby that she's named Chairman

Meow. "They're totally adorable!"

I should pause here for a moment to tell you about these treecats. They aren't cats, although they do look a bit feline with their triangular faces, big eyes, and lithe furred bodies. They're about that size too. But their legs are more like a koala's, built for climbing trees—or *anything*. We found them on a planet halfway up the Beta Aurigae spur.

It was the turn of our chief engineer at the time, Saul, to name the planet, and he chose Leaves-A-Million. Then when we were heading back into orbit, emptyhanded, or so we thought, half a dozen furry alien beasties tumbled out of the pantry, and Saul retrospectively changed the name of the planet to Sphinx, and named them treecats. He was a huge science fiction fan, always shoving books and films at you.

Saul used to say that sci-fi died in 2024, which was when the Interstellar Railroad zoomed out of the sky. Now the galaxy is ours, and the riches of bygone civilizations are there for the picking up. People still talk about the Star Trek dream, but the "boldly go" jokes wear thin after you've lost enough friends. And there's no peace to be made with aliens when they're all dead.

However, their loss is our gain. As we whirl out towards Omega Centauri, following the taillights of Finian's fleet, I feel the old excitement sparking up again. Who knows what we might find out here? We're heading for the frontier. Finian's hinted at a mighty trove of A-tech lying in wait. Maybe he's stumbled on the ruins of an alien empire no one's discovered yet. Maybe he's found *live* aliens—ones that have discovered the secret of eternal life!

Well, that's not likely. But is it unrealistic that I might find something small enough to fit in my pocket?

Just one little find, that's all I need.

One find that isn't shite.

It has famously happened that more than one explorer walked straight past something a sharper-eyed soul later sold for millions. You're looking for the secret of eternal life, say, and so you ignore the queer little cocktail umbrellas stuck in the ground everywhere, which turn out to optimize biological nitrogen fixation. That patent went for $480,000,000 to Archer Daniels Midland. You've got to keep an open mind.

The treecats are a classic example of what happens when you *don't* keep an open mind. Saul and Harriet both insisted at first that they were sentient. Bollocks to that, says I. Calling an animal a treecat does not make it a sophont capable of telepathically bonding with a human. (I read part of that book at Saul's urging.) It just makes it an animal with a catchy name. Harriet eventually concluded they are about as smart as colobus monkeys. But by that time, we were six hundred lightyears away, and it was too late to drop the treecats off on their home planet, even though there turned out to be *seventeen* of them.

"They have got one promising characteristic," I say to Imogen, a month or so into our voyage.

"What's that?"

The two of us are alone on the bridge. Now that she's taken over piloting duties, I'm back to being the chief A-tech scout, which means there's not much for me to do at the moment. There's not much for her to do, either. The Railroad stretches away forever through the blackness of mysteriously folded space. The taillights of the *Big Swinging Dick*, one of Finian's new ships, glow ahead like red eyes.

Imogen touches the yoke from time to time to maintain our trim, as the *Bogtrotter's* antique inertial dampeners shift 500 tons of cargo around. She's got 'her' treecat, named Fluffington, on her lap.

"Nice moggy," I croon, reaching out to tickle Fluffington behind the ears. "I think you like me really. Don't you?" I think no such thing. This is just a pretext to move closer to Imogen, and Fluffington seems to see through it, because he nips my arm with his eight million pointy teeth. "OW!"

Imogen frowns at me. "So what exactly have they got going for them?"

"They're kleptomaniacs."

Her expression brightens. "Oh my God, they totally are! Fluffie's got the craziest shit in his nest. Spoons, wires, I don't even know what."

"Yeah, the Captain lost his iPhone on the Beta Aurigae spur. It finally turned up last week in Chairman Meow's nest."

"I'm not surprised. Fluffie's like a magpie—if it's sparkly, he wants it. He even got into my safe the other day, which is like, OK, how the *hell* did you manage that?" She strokes him lovingly. I am jealous.

"Imogen, would it be out of line to ask what you've got in that safe?" I am fairly sure it's the same one she used to cart about when she was selling jewelry on commission for the Arcadian mob.

She slants a wary glance at me. The bridge is quiet, for once, apart from the humming of the computers. Gordon's dragged Donal off to teach him about finance, so we haven't got to listen to his music. It's just Imogen and me and the Interstellar Railroad. I wish this could go on forever.

I feel a sense of peace when I'm with her. It's like being alone, without the alone part.

"You know, I used to sell jewelry," she says. "So … I kind of took a few of my favorite pieces. Most of it was just bling. But we had some A-tech pendants with wireless comms functionality, and … stuff. I liked those." She shrugs. "So I took them."

I laugh out loud. "You'll never eat lunch on Arcadia again."

"I know. This trip better work out."

I want to grab her and kiss her. I heroically restrain myself. Fluffington growls.

Donal strolls onto the bridge and leers, believing that he has interrupted a romantic moment. I *wish*. He casts an eye over the screens that Imogen and I have been ignoring. "Hey, we've got a capsule from the *Big Swinging Dick*!"

"That sounds so wrong," Imogen mutters.

These capsules are the only way to communicate ship-to-ship when you're on the Railroad. Radios don't work up here—well, I suppose technically they do, but you'd be old and gray by the time you got through how-are-things, I'm-surviving. The *Big Swinging Dick* is dozens of lightyears away, even if we can see her taillights. So they've sent us a message capsule. Similar to mail packets, these little efforts are cylinders with chain dogs on the bottom. Drop them on the rails and shoot them back to the other party. So much for peace and quiet.

I clatter downstairs with Donal to retrieve the *BSD's* message. The *Intergalactic Bogtrotter* being military surplus and about as old as I am, it doesn't have one of those handy robotic arms that can grab a capsule and bring it inside.

Someone has to suit up and go out and fetch it. Donal starts to get into the old EVA suit we keep down here, but I stop him. I have this recurring fear that if he once gets into a suit of *any* kind, we'll never get him out of it again. It's irrational, I know. Ruby, who tried to kill him on Planet Suckass, is five ships down the line, and in the middle of transitioning to female. Donal's got no reason to fear for his life …

… and yet, and yet.

I put the spacesuit on.

Outside the ship, I keep my tether short and slide the magnetic soles of my boots over the hull. The Railroad whips past 'below' my head. I fight zero-gee nausea. I detest spacewalking.

A gandy dancer pokes its head around the curve of the hull and holds out the capsule, blank-faced.

"Thanks," I mutter, knowing it can't hear me. I take the capsule from the stubby three-fingered hand.

The gandy dancers came with the Railroad. They're humanoid, with bulgy heads, you'd recognize them from all those supermarket tabloid pictures in the 20th and early 21st centuries. The belief is they were testing us for sentience at that time, and somehow we passed. They try to be helpful. For this reason among others, it's thought that they're not actually alive. They're energy-based automatons built by the same long-gone entities that built the Railroad. Probably.

The gandy dancer vanishes, and I scuttle gladly back into the ship.

Donal opens the capsule. "It's from Finian …"

This is SOP. Since the *Marauding Elephant* is in point position, Finian has to pass his messages back from one ship to the next. Each captain adds comments along the way, e.g.:

- *Pit stop, next exit —Finian*
- *About time —David* (captain of the *Avenging Angel,* a stupidly up-armored Boeing X-90)
- *Did anyone remember to bring the barbie? —Jennifer* (captain of the *Bond Girl*)
- *It might be in the supply ship —Armando* (captain of the *Terremoto.* I hate his Spanish guts. The supply ship, indeed.)
- *Have a look for it, Donal, if you don't mind —Willem* (Dutch, 5'2", named his ship the *Big Swinging Dick*; some people are beyond mockery)

So Donal goes to search for the barbecue grill, and I warn everyone to secure any loose objects and treecats, and fasten their seatbelts in preparation for landing. I'm such a comedian.

CHAPTER 5

We come off the Railroad behind the *Big Swinging Dick* and join the rest of the fleet in orbit around a turquoise and green planet. The radio's alive with cross-talk, crews exchanging long-hoarded insults. Finian directs us to land on the edge of the largest continent on the planet's dayside.

"This planet's mine," he boasts over the radio. "I call it the Burren."

The Burren, if you're not aware, is a scenic region in the west of County Clare. The name turns out to be quite apt. Just like its namesake, Planet Burren, or this region of it anyway, is windy, treeless, and a dead loss in economic terms. We land our ships on the cracked, grassy pavement of glacial rocks that clearly inspired the planet's name, and hurry towards the sea. Surf curls onto a wide shingle beach. The real Burren hasn't got *that*. I soon discover another difference: the sea here is deliciously warm.

If you've never seen 93 pirates, many of them past retirement age, in their swimming togs, you're not missing much. But the sea is large, the sky is huge, and their voices fade as I swim out deep. I float on my back. Ah, solitude.

Then I get stung by something that looks like floating Brillo, and when I flounder back to shore everyone cracks up at the weals on my back. It's a good thing I got my booster shot before we left Arcadia. These immune boosters we get are A-tech, fecking amazing—we can laugh off alien toxins and infections that would've felled a whole crew in Finian's day.

"I was first out in this way in '33," Finian says, reminding us all how old he is. "We were prancing round in EVA suits back then, of course. It was the days before booster shots. No swimming, no sunbathing. But even through a triple-strength faceplate and a layer of Kevlar, I knew I wanted to come back someday."

We are sweating in the sun, shifting cargo from the *Bogtrotter* to the five other ships, which are parked as close together as is safe, given that their engines char a wide area when landing and taking off. We're redistributing food and water across the fleet, giving each ship sufficient provisions for another month on the Railroad. I still can't work out why Finian's so keen to fly nonstop from here on out. For that matter we could have filled the water tanks from the Burren's sea. We've got desalination equipment. But Finian made vague noises about wanting to get on as fast as possible.

So we're jogging 500 yards between one ship and the next, following anti-grav gliders loaded with stuff—and Finian, who's taking his ease on top of the rice and potatoes and mountains of spare batteries.

"I came back in '56, when I had my own ship," he reminisces.

You'll notice he's glossed over the years *I* spent on that

ship, on the Draco Spur. That did not end very well for Finian. I've only heard the story at second hand, as he'd booted me off his crew by then, but the way my dad heard it from Padraig, who's one of Finian's trusted men, Finian got into a full-scale battle with another *cough cough* 'explorer,' and the other fella kicked his arse for him. No wonder he fled to the other side of the galaxy after that, and no wonder he doesn't mention it now.

"I claimed this place as fast as I could drop a beacon," he says. This is how you claim planets: you drop beacons on them with your ID and the date, and hope some fecker doesn't come along and move the beacon before you can get back to Earth and file an official claim with the Planetary Registration. You've got to pay through the nose for that, of course.

"After that, I carried on up the Omega Centauri spur, claiming everything with water on it. By God, lads, there are some jewels up there! Views you've got to see to believe. And ..." Finian sits up and surveys the rest of us flocking behind the gliders. "The reason we're here. On a certain planet, I made an absolutely fecking stunning discovery."

"Go on Finian, don't keep us in suspense," cries Jennifer of the *Bond Girl.*

"Heh heh," he cackles. "I want to see your face when we get there, darlin'."

The thought crosses my mind that there's got to be *some* reason Finian did not claim this 'stunning' discovery nine years ago. But I'm hot and tired and I could eat the hind leg off the Lamb of God.

"We've got time to fire up the barbie, anyway," Finian says.

The *Bond Girl's* cook takes charge of grilling duties. When you want a barbecue done right, leave it to the Australians. The steaks and burgers may have started off frozen, but they come off the grill sizzling and flavorsome. There's coleslaw, and fresh bread, and a platter of shrimp which Ruby carries around like a cocktail waitress, offering it with a simper. He's even got a little apron and a doily on his head. Donal and I have a laugh about that.

"I can't believe I was ever scared of him," Donal says.

"Her, Donal, *her.* Mind your pronouns."

We sit around the campfire stuffing our faces as the sun slides towards the sea. Donal's got his arm around Harriet. Kenneth (the lazy dosser, he didn't even offer to help with the grill; I don't believe he was a cook any more than he was a pilot) has got his hand up Vanessa's t-shirt. I am sitting next to Imogen and I have *not* got my hand up her t-shirt. It's the only flaw in an otherwise perfect cookout, 3.1 kiloparsecs from Earth.

Finian drones on between gulps of lager. When he's speaking there can be no other conversation, except on the fringes (remember there are 106 of us) where the lesser pirates are squabbling in their various languages. Everyone in the English-speaking circle leans towards Finian, and oohs and aahs in the right places because he's *Finian,* the $700 Million Man. I am deliberately ignoring him, for the principle of the thing, when a sudden shift in the pitch of his voice captures my attention.

"—and then they attacked us! Out of a blue sky, they swooped down upon us with five upgraded DC-100s and thousands of homemade flitter-bombers. They strafed our camp, killed half of my men on their first pass …"

What, what?

"… we ran for the ships …"

I frantically nudge Donal. "What's he on about?"

"Just listen!" Donal leans forward as if a string is pulling him towards the demonic form sat gesticulating on the other side of the campfire.

"I personally notched up eleven kills," Finian brags. "Those rotten little flitter-bombers are lethal, to the man flying them. A shit sandwich with A-tech bells and whistles is still a shit sandwich. But in the end we had to retreat. We were outnumbered five to one, in terms of actual ships…"

Listening with intense interest now, I piece together the story wrapped in Finian's exaggerations and digressions.

The short version is we're fecked.

The long version is we're completely fecked, and here's why:

When he first travelled up the Omega Centauri spur, nine years ago, Finian somehow neglected to consider the possibility that he was being followed. He was, and the other fellas were cleverer than him. They hung back, waiting for him to find something good. When he did—they deduced this when he settled in for a month's stay on this 'certain planet' of his—they swooped in to grab the loot.

This is a time-honored exploration tactic. You don't *have* to have sharp eyes or an open mind. You just have to have bigger guns. Needless to say it is illegal to kill people, burn their ships, and claim their discoveries as your own. However, there are no police out here. So the further you get from Earth, the better your odds of feeling alien worm-analogs, while some other bastard laughs all the way to the bank.

Having powerful backers, like we did with the *Skint Idjit,* improves your chances. Even pirates will be deterred by the prospect of Goldman Sachs dragging them into court.

But Finian has never deigned to take a penny from 'The Establishment.' So he was very lucky to get away from the Omega Centauri spur with his life.

And now he's taking five heavily armed ships, plus one *Intergalactic Bogtrotter, back,* to teach the feckers a lesson?!?

"I give up," I say to Imogen. I have gone for a walk to relieve my feelings, and she's come after me. That would be encouraging, if I were in any state of mind to appreciate it. "Jesus and Mary! I just give up."

She squints out to sea. The twilight is luminous here. The sky seems to glow with an inner light. "Well, the guys who attacked him must be dead by now," she says. "I mean, if they ever made it back, it would've been all over the news, if this discovery is as big as he says it is."

She's parroting Finian's own logic. Oh, I suppose they *might* be dead. Alien wildlife, bad weather, radiation, fuel shortages, drunken brawls—on the Interstellar Railroad, there's no shortage of health hazards. Six million ways to die? Try thirty billion.

"So we'll just stroll in and pick up the A-tech," Finian said before I left the campfire, and everyone cheered.

But I know my uncle better than they do. He did not come all this way for A-tech. He already *had* three-quarters of a billion dollars, before he spent it on this lot! No, there is only one thing that could bring Finian Connolly back to the Omega Centauri spur at his time of life, and that is a grudge.

"If he really thinks they're dead," I say, "why did he wait

so long to come back?"

"To be on the safe side?" Imogen says.

"With this huge discovery lying around, waiting to be found by someone else? No, he waited until he was rich enough to hire a fleet of like-minded arseholes—*and not one minute longer*. The instant he got that cheque for $700 million, he was off like a hare."

"But why would he need a whole fleet?" she says.

I grind my teeth. "Because he thinks they're still there, and he wants to blow them to shite, of course. And now he's dragged us into it!"

I almost said *dragged YOU into it*. She wouldn't like that. She's not the sort of woman to want protecting. But the fact remains, if she gets hurt because I convinced, nay, begged her to take this job, I'll feel extremely bad.

"There's only one thing for it," I say. "We'll have to grab his A-tech discovery out from under his nose, while he's busy piling into the competition."

"You really think you can beat him at his own game," she says skeptically.

"Darlin', I'm a great believer in try, try, try again," I say, smiling. She doesn't smile. She stares into my eyes, and I stare back at her. The sunset is a golden explosion.

Donal comes up beside us. The man's got an incomparable sense of timing. He's too upset to notice. "So who do you think they are?"

"Who?" Imogen says.

I know what he means. *Who* drove Finian off A Certain Planet, nine years ago? Finian gave out he never identified them, but he was talking shite. Wankers like that plaster their names all over their second-hand Fed-Ex cargo jets.

"It's got to be Special Delivery Sam," I say.

"That's what I was thinking," Donal says.

"Who?" Imogen says, a trifle irritated.

"Special Delivery Sam," I repeat. "That was the fella who handed Finian's arse to him on the Draco spur. He used to be a pilot for Fed-Ex. That's how he got the name. But don't make the mistake of underestimating him."

"Jeez, I wouldn't," Imogen says with a shudder. "I used to be a taxi driver. The delivery service guys were the worst."

The sun completes its plunge into the sea. The sky gets *brighter*. It's not dark. It is stars from horizon to horizon. It's like looking up into the heart of the galaxy.

Of course, Planet Burren is on the edge of Omega Centauri.

What a fantastic view!

On the spur of the moment, I slide an arm around Imogen's waist.

She's trembling.

It's not *that* cold.

Pointing upwards, she squeaks, "Are those stars meant to be moving?"

The last words are swallowed in a string of sonic booms.

CHAPTER 6

"To the ships!" Finian howls. "To the ships!"

You don't have to tell me twice, big fella.

This must be excruciating for him. Special Delivery Sam caught him flatfooted on the ground once before, and now he's done it again, if I don't miss my guess, and I seldom do when it's a matter of assuming the worst.

The enemy ships scream over and away, trailing thunderclaps as they break the sound barrier. One of them banks over the sea and I see the logo on its fuselage, painted with the same A-tech paint Donal used for the *Bogtrotter's* name, so it glows in the dark. It's the Fed-Ex logo, same colors, except it says *Sam-I-Am*.

Two fiery fountains gout up from the Burren into the star-filled sky. A double-barrelled boom crashes over us, sound following light.

Mother of God, their aim is horrible.

We scatter in blind panic. It looks like the ships hit were the two parked furthest from our campsite, the *Bond Girl* and the *Terremoto*. The *Bogtrotter's* silhouette towers intact against the night, thank God. I sprint towards her, mindful of the cracks in the glacial-era pavement. Donal and I did a lot of running away during our adolescent years, which you might argue have not ended, heh heh. We may not be that fleet of foot anymore but we know a few tricks. I trip the fella behind me, knocking him sprawling, and five more fall over him. We reach the steps of the *Bogtrotter* before anyone else does.

Then hell reigns around us, ash blowing from the fireballs a mile off, the smell of carbonizing chemicals on the wind, people rushing the steps of the *Bogtrotter*. Donal zooms upstairs to initiate our emergency accelerated launch countdown. I hold the bottom of the steps, shoving our crew upstairs one after the other, and kicking anyone else who tries it. A couple of Spaniards are arguing violently with my admittance policy when the South Africans turn up and take over from me. No one's getting past *them*.

At the top of the stairs I glance back at the beach. Finian's still standing by the campfire, a shaggy-headed silhouette, literally shaking his fists at the luminescent sky. Bleeding idjit.

He shouldn't be dying here. It's not right. I want to go back for him and drag him aboard the *Bogtrotter*. But it's too far to the beach. I wouldn't make it there and back, and then I remember how he cheated me out of $280 million, and I duck into the airlock.

Gordon and Imogen are in. A few minutes later, the slam of the airlock resounds through the ship. The South Africans tumble on to the bridge. "That's everyone," says Hendrik, his face war-painted with ash.

"OK," Imogen says, her voice shrill with tension. "Now I am going to show you some *real* flying."

Hardly are the words out of her mouth when the enemy ships thunder back for another go at us. We all freeze, waiting to turn into clouds of radioactive atoms. Except Imogen. By the time I realize I'm still alive, I am sprawling on the floor.

"Excelsior!" Imogen cries. "Hold onto your hats!"

The *Intergalactic Bogtrotter* lofts into the air. I scramble to the navigation station and peer at the screens. *Three* fiery torches now burn upon the Burren. When a nuclear-powered spaceship blows up, it's not the reactor that makes the fireworks. *That* just melts. It's all the liquid hydrogen propellant.

The enemy ships wink at us, zooming back over the ocean. Each wink is a laser beam scoring our shielding.

"Bite me, douchebags!" Imogen screams. She yanks back on the yoke, and the *Bogtrotter* goes into a near-vertical climb.

Have you ever seen a third-hand Lockheed-Martin F-99 go head to head with six second-hand Fed-Ex cargo planes?

No, neither have I, for Imogen leaves them gulping our rocket exhaust. The *Bogtrotter* may be old, but she's got a 2.3 GW reactor under the hood, and thanks to Gordon's fine-tuning, the reactor can now deliver all 23,000,000,000 of those watts to the thrusters. We scream away from the Burren at escape velocity.

Halfway into orbit, Shaka remembers that we have guns. "We should give them a goodbye present!"

"Sit down, you fecking nutter," Donal says coldly.

Two minutes later, I hear the beautiful, beautiful sound of our chain dogs clamping onto the local loop.

"Which way, Captain?" Imogen says, not taking her eyes

off her screens. "Junction coming up in eighteen … seventeen …"

Donal glances at me.

There are certain things the captain of an exploration ship can't say. So I say it for him. "Back the way we came!"

Back to safety, back to civilization. Back to a $50 million debt, and everyone blaming us for leaving Finian to die. I should have bailed on this business when I had the chance.

"There's a ship in the junction!" Imogen shouts.

Headlights blaze from the screens, so bright they white out the Railroad ahead. The other ship is racing towards the junction, too.

It's on the track we wanted to take, the one that leads back to Arcadia.

"Which way?" Imogen shouts. "Captain?"

Donal gapes feebly at the screens. There's no question of *which way* anymore. The only open track is the Omega Centauri spur. But which ship will reach the junction first?

"Put the pedal to the floor, Gordon," begs a desperate chorus, me included.

Closer, closer, we're all going to die—

Chain dogs screaming, the *Bogtrotter* shoots through the junction under the other ship's nose. The screens go dark.

We bowl at top speed onto the Omega Centauri spur.

Into the unknown.

I peer at the rearview screen. "Oh, look. They're coming after us. Isn't that grand."

Donal throws me an angry look. Then he pukes all over the floor.

CHAPTER 7

We thought it was radiation poisoning, from those exploding ships, and Harriet made us all take rad pills. But Donal was the only one who developed any symptoms. A day later he's still alternately puking and running to the loo.

"It must have been the shrimp," he says weakly.

Meanwhile, I've made the shattering discovery that our crew has *tripled* in number.

We now have eight Spaniards on board, including Armando, the captain of the *Terremoto,* and three-quarters of the crew of the *Bond Girl.*

So much for my belief that no one could get past the South Africans.

"This big girl's blouse," I say, pushing Hendrik at Donal, "let them on board after I went upstairs."

"You didn't say not to," Hendrik grumbles.

"It was implied, you twat!"

Donal looks up, pale, sweat standing on his forehead. He's sat on the loo with his kecks around his ankles. "That was really fecking stupid, Henny," he grits.

"They lost their ships," Hendrik says, getting

self-righteous. "You want to leave them to die? That's inhuman, man."

The smell is appalling. I close the door of the loo, shutting Donal in with his pain. "You may have forgotten," I say quietly to Hendrik, "we offloaded eighty percent of the supplies on the Burren. We've got enough food and water for a month, for *us*. Not for thirty-seven."

And Special Delivery Sam's thugs are breathing down our bumper.

They've kept up the pursuit for a solid thirty hours and they show no sign of slackening their pace. Their headlights shine into the bridge from the rearview screen, fraying everyone's nerves.

Shaka argues for coming off the Railroad at the next planet, luring them into pursuit, and shooting them to bits.

Armando the Bucanero backs him up. The nosey bleeder has been poking about belowdecks and has discovered that the *Bogtrotter's* railguns are in working order, to say nothing of her laser batteries. We should have decommissioned all this stuff on Arcadia, in compliance with commercial shipping law, but you know how it is, you've got a thousand things to do and some of them never get done.

So theoretically, the *Bogtrotter* is as deadly as ever the *Hellraiser* was, and the South Africans are clamoring at me to have a go.

I decline, for the following reasons:

1) Who's to say there is only one ship pursuing us? Just because we can only see one does not mean there aren't six more piled up behind it. The Railroad is straight, straight, straight.

2) Special Delivery Sam clearly thinks of the Omega

Centauri cluster as his private empire. That means he'll have a ship or three stationed on every planet along this spur. Wherever we come off, we might end up trapped between them and the pursuit.

3)   I don't want to die.

Reason #3 should go without saying. But the terryfing truth is it doesn't with this crowd. Be they Spaniards, Australians, or nice middle-class South African boys, there are far too many men (they are usually men) who take to the Railroad to play the game with maximum panache, not to win at the end of it. I'd have hoped Finian would have winnowed these dangerous bleeders out during the hiring process. But if he was fishing in the piratical end of the talent pool, I'd imagine it was near-impossible to find crews motivated exclusively by honest greed. Even we didn't manage it, and Donal made it clear from the start, back when we were hiring Hendrik and his lads, that there'd be no death-defying escapades.

Funny how these things work out.

I drag Gordon down to the crew quarters— "You've got to get some sleep." By an evil stroke of luck, none of our Spanish and Australian stowaways were their ship's stacker. So it's all on Gordon's shoulders.

"I've got to stay on watch," he says.

"No, you don't. All we're doing is running in a straight line."

Back at the back of the ship where the cabins are, you can hear the roar of the turbines, a noise that always bothers me when I'm trying to get to sleep, although I've not had much chance to do that lately.

"How far are we going to run, Fletcher?" Gordon says

quietly. "Through the Omega Centauri cluster and out the other side?"

"How big is this cluster, anyway?" It seems a good time to ask.

"It contains an estimated ten million stars."

"And it's how wide?"

"A hundred and fifty lightyears, give or take."

"And what's on the other side?"

"No one knows," Gordon says, and he gets a dreamy look on his face. "Whirlpools? Dragons? Elephants riding on the backs of giant turtles? The Total Perspective Vortex? I suppose we'll find out."

Not if I've got anything to do with it, we won't. I guide Gordon into his cabin. He's got one to himself, as befits his age and indispensability. He sits down on his bed and I sit down at his computer desk.

"I want to find this planet of Finian's," I say.

"This isn't a lark anymore, Fletcher."

"It never was!" I shout at him. "My uncle's dead! Shot down in cold blood by a fecking postman! If you think I'm going to run away with my tail between my legs, you don't know the Connollys."

It *was* a lark to Gordon, I know. Retired from his high-flying job in finance, touring the galaxy with Finian's disreputable crew, he was having a high old time. Maybe now he's started to see this game for what it is—teeth and nails and devil take the hindmost.

"I think you'd sell your own granny for a big A-tech discovery," he says to me now.

Damn him and his 200+ IQ.

"That's not what it's about, Fletch."

"Do tell me what it's about, in your opinion," I say between my teeth.

"Exploration, you dunce! Like it says on the tin! Expanding the boundaries of human knowledge. Building up redundancy for our species. Transitioning to a true galactic civilization, before we stumble on the *wrong* planet and push the *wrong* button and destroy ourselves, like every last gang of sentient idiots before us!"

It's his turn to shout at me. I blink at him for a second, impressed by his passion. Then I lean forward. "You think maybe this planet of Finian's is the wrong one, eh? And Special Delivery Sam's out here searching for the big red button? Or maybe he's already found it?"

Gordon shakes his head wearily.

"Good," I say, standing up. "Because I wouldn't want to destroy the galaxy on top of everything." I lean down to him. "C'mon, where's this planet, Gordon? You were here with Finian in '56. You must know."

Returning to the bridge, I glad-hand the odds and sods. "Forty-ninth exit from the Burren. We're coming off." Oh Jesus, am I mad? Probably. But somewhere Finian's ghost is smiling.

Anyway, the alternative is running straight through the Omega Centauri cluster and out the other side, and Gordon may think that's a fine idea, but I beg to differ. I'd rather take my chances on Omega Centauri 49.

I turn to Shaka. "Well, hotshot? Now's your chance to show what you can do. Go see about those guns."

Shaka and the other South Africans fly downstairs with cries of joy.

Ignoring questions from Imogen, I check the exit counter

Gordon set up at the navigation station. The stars, and hence the habitable planets, are so close together in the Omega Centauri cluster that they're flying by at a rate of one every twenty minutes. We've just passed the forty-third exit since the Burren. Perfect. I'll let Gordon sleep for an hour or two, and then ...

Armando the Bucanero, hovering behind Imogen, lets out a screech. *"Me cago en Dios!"*

"What? What?"

He points over Imogen's shoulder at the screen showing the Railroad.

Twin stars twinkle, far ahead.

No. You can't see any stars on the Railroad. Those are the lights of an approaching ship.

CHAPTER 8

The ship races towards us, and my scalp freezes with terror.

The Interstellar Railroad is, of course, two-way. It looks like an old Earth railroad, with the parallel rails and the crossties between them. But your chain dogs only clamp onto one rail, so there's room for another ship to pass you on the other rail, going the other way.

It doesn't *look* like there's room, but there always is, no matter how wide your ship might be. They've experimented with mile long container ships turned sideways.

Oh, and it doesn't matter which rail you were on to start with. If some idjit is rushing headlong at you on the same rail, you'll still squeeze past each other at many times the speed of light.

Yes, those long-dead aliens who built the Railroad were clever ... but they were not clever enough to anticipate human viciousness. Or maybe they were, who knows, maybe us killing each other was all part of their master plan.

For the Railroad folds spacetime, but it *exists* in real space, so it follows that when you're passing another ship, there is a picosecond of time when you're infinitely close to it, and you can unload a broadside of laser pulses or even kinetics, if your gunnery computer's precise enough, at point blank range.

This is why every tactically capable ship in the universe has its laser batteries on its sides.

The *Intergalactic Bogtrotter* does too.

But Shaka, who'd be our gunner, has just gone downstairs to prep the railguns for a completely different type of contact, and there's no time to summon him back.

Armando dashes for the empty gunner's couch, gibbering in Spanish.

I kick him in the hamstrings. He goes down with a crack, hitting his chin on the deck.

I drop into the gunner's couch, enter Donal's password, and command the computer to rake the approaching ship with laser fire at the instant of closest approach. No human being can get the timing right at these speeds, although I know Armando would have tried. He's spitting blood, calling me a *hijo de puta*.

The lights of the oncoming ship blaze into the bridge. "Oh my God oh MY GOD," Imogen screams. She curls up in a ball, hiding her face. It's the first time I've ever seen her lose her cool.

I sprawl loose-limbed in the gunner's couch, feeling weirdly detached from everything.

Thunderous impacts slam into the *Bogtrotter* with the force of a car crash. Everyone who was standing up falls down, and everyone who was seated falls out of their couch.

I stumble upright amid screeching alarms and strobing emergency lights.

Donal hurtles onto the bridge, doing up his belt, yelling,

"What happened?!?"

"They used kinetics," I say. I can taste blood in my mouth.

"We're losing power to the chain dogs," Imogen shrieks. She's back on her feet, hauling on the yoke, which seems to have got stuck in the hard-a-port position. "Gordon where's Gordon HE NEEDS TO GET HERE!"

The alarms are telling us we're losing pressurization. The emergency pressure doors all over the ship have sealed. Even if Gordon is still alive, he's stuck in the crew quarters.

Donal calmly reviews the alerts, and initiates an emergency shutdown of the reactor.

"Somebody fucking help me," Imogen screams.

So we all haul on her as she hauls on the yoke. What a bunch of monkeys.

Ten seconds later, the *Bogtrotter* swoons off the Railroad into uncharted interstellar space.

CHAPTER 9

Interstellar space in the Omega Centauri cluster is not what you think of when you think of the vastness of the universe.

Starlight floods the bridge. Every screen shows stars as bright as Sirius, amidst a milky haze of more-distant stars. It's bright enough to work by, like reading by the light of the telly in a dark room. Not that I'm doing any work. None of us are.

Gordon has diverted every erg of stored power to the thrusters, so the inertial dampeners are off, and we're all drifting around in freefall, saying sorry when we bump into each other.

Have I mentioned I hate freefall? I've already puked once.

"There's a large gravitational attractor ahead," Gordon says over the intercom.

He survived the depressurization of the crew quarters by whipping on the spacesuit that he keeps under his bed at all times. He's still in his cabin, working on his laptop, which is hooked up to the *Bogtrotter's* control systems.

"Imogen, can you see the object I'm describing?" he says.

"Yes," she whispers. "It looks like a planet."

I swim through the air, using other people as handles. The object on the viewscreen is round, dark, and about the size of my fist held at arm's length. Starlight illuminates one curve.

"What's a planet doing all the way out here?" Kenneth voices the question that's in my own mind.

Gordon crackles, "I would theorize that it hasn't been here long. A galactic cluster is a busy neighborhood. A passing star may have ripped this planet away from its sun, flinging it into space. The other possibility is that it's a rogue planet, but those are generally gas giants. This one looks terrestrial, perhaps even habitable—which is a stroke of luck for us."

Gordon is a master of understatement.

"We'll set down there if we can," Donal says.

Support for this decision is unanimous, since the alternative is perishing in deep space when our air runs out.

But it takes so *long* to get there! The Interstellar Railroad has spoiled us. We expect to skip from planet to planet in a few hours plus time-to-orbit. We've lost the knack of sitting, sorry, *floating* around patiently for weeks on end, in a tin can that would be a tight squeeze for four people, never mind nine, which is how many were on the bridge at the moment of the attack.

The worst part of it is listening to the others die.

Gordon stumps around the parts of the ship that are now in vacuum, delivering encouragement and EVA suits. He rescues the four South Africans who got stuck in the ammo locker, so now there are five people stumping around in spacesuits. But there is nothing any of them can do for the seven Australians, two Spaniards, and two more South Africans who were stranded in their cabins at the time of the attack. Those cabins are boxes with bunks in. They're meant to hold pressurization for long enough for you to get into your EVA suit. If you don't have an EVA suit, you're toast.

Three of them commit suicide before the end.

As for the other stowaways, they were all killed instantly in the attack.

So we're more or less back to our original strength, which would help with rationing, except that there is NO FOOD on the bridge. All right, I exaggerate. There is a stash of MREs that are nine years past their best before dates. The *Hellraiser's* original crew must have inherited them from the USAF.

We drink the water from the toilet.

And I think that gives you a good enough idea of what it's like, so I'll gloss over Day 5, when Armando and his sole surviving companero get into a fight with Kenneth about who took the last packet of Pork Chow Mein. Kenneth blames the treecats, and Vanessa backs him up, and Harriet defends the treecats, and Donal attempts to make peace, and I *may* have shoved Armando in the back at the very moment he was threatening to cut Kenneth's balls off.

The end result is both Spaniards wind up with their blood on the outside of their bodies.

We do *not* eat them.

The treecats do.

So it's a wretched crew, seething with hatred and self-pity, that guides the *Bogtrotter* down to the surface of the Lost Planet on Day 7.

We land on an icy, starlit plain near one of the weird objects we saw from orbit, which have been consuming the 0.01% of our attention not devoted to food-related matters. These are shaped like halves of golf balls. They're city-sized, mountain-high, and you can't take anything for granted with aliens, but they look like domes to me.

Sitting on the ice, we observe movement at the foot of the nearest dome. Something is coming out and going back in, twice a day—twice an *Earth* day, that is. The Lost Planet has no sun, hence no days at all.

But we have to contain our curiosity for 40 more hours, while Gordon and the four South Africans work to free us from the bridge. They survived in their EVA suits all this time by taking turns to rest, eat, and sleep on the control deck, which has its own airlock. But their refuge is separated from ours by vacuum. And there's a gaping hole in the hull right outside the bridge. That has to be sealed before this part of the ship can be repressurized. We don't have enough carbonfoam, so they end up sealing the hole with *ice,* which is not as mad as it sounds, given that the temperature outside is down in the minus 100 range.

At last we stumble forth into the arms of four South African desperadoes and one septuagenarian pirate, and I would weep for joy if it wasn't so fecking cold. Our breath clouds the new-made air in the corridor.

"The surface of a sunless planet should be much colder than this," Gordon tuts. "A great deal of heat is being expelled from those domes. They're probably using the same mass-energy conversion system that was found on Deneb 3b, among other planets. The construction of the domes certainly evokes the Denebite Empire ..."

The Denebite Empire is old hat. They had four arms and beaks for faces, and they colonized most of the Carina-Sagittarius spiral arm.

If Gordon's right, and this is a 5-million-year-old Denebite outpost, there's nothing new to be found here. But at the moment I don't care. Our rescuers have brought some long-shelf-life pastries and Clonakilty black puddings up from the kitchen. The stuff is freeze-dried by a week in vacuum. We tear into it so eagerly that we're at risk of losing teeth.

When we start to get frostbite, we stop eating and scramble into our spacesuits. After the debacle on the *Skint Idjit,* Donal insisted on having enough spacesuits to go around this time. They're third-hand, and smell like knickers, but that's the sweetest perfume compared to the smell on the bridge these past days.

Harriet and Imogen fuss over the treecats. Ten of the little beasts survive. Gordon, who has also fallen for their cuteness, went to the bother of bringing their pressurized cat carriers up from the cargo hold, so they can survive a bit longer.

Lugging the treecats, we tramp across the plain. Gordon explains that the layer of squeaky snow underfoot used to be the Lost Planet's atmosphere. The stars are so big and close, it's as bright as day.

It's very strange to look up at the sky and see no local loop of the Railroad. That thin glowing band is always there, on every habitable planet. Its absence is a crushing reminder that the Lost Planet is not habitable.

We'll just have to pray this dome has some resources to offer.

Walking in a spacesuit is horrible at the best of times. I get hot and sweaty and the dome seems to come no nearer, until finally I look up from the pitted snow, and there it is.

Too tired to speak, we stare up at the mysterious structure. It's made of some silicate A-tech material. There is no visible door. If this is a dead end, we're finished.

Gordon—easily identifiable in his Old Elephant spacesuit—steps forward and picks something up. A transparent ball. It's a bit smaller than a football. He throws it into the air. It floats slowly back to the ground.

"Damn it all to bloody hell!" he shouts, and lashes out with a kick.

Dozens more of the bubbles rise around him.

There are hundreds, *millions* of these bubbles piled around the base of the dome. We plunge into them like kids into a ball pool. They're squashy and fun to land on. They look like the bubbles you used to blow with washing-up liquid when you were little, but they don't break. I throw an armful at Imogen, and she throws more back. For a few moments the radio crackles with our laughter. I almost forget we're 3.5 kiloparsecs from home and about to die of hunger and cold.

Then a house-sized section of the dome slides up.

A robot dumper truck drives out and upends its skip.

Thousands *more* squashy bubbles cascade onto the plain.

Indifferent to us, the truck drives away a few hundred yards. It deploys two scoop arms and fills its now-empty skip with snow. We all watch, drop-jawed. What it's doing is boring and beside the point. It *moves,* that's the point. A-tech that's still working after all these years always sends shivers up your spine.

"Yes, almost certainly Denebite," Gordon says. "The curvilinear wheelbase is a giveaway."

Full of snow, the dumper truck drives back to the hole in the dome. It's halfway inside when—

"Wait!"

I hurl myself at the truck.

The sides of the skip are too high to climb. I get my elbows over the top. Struggling, I feel like I'm thirteen again, back in Lisdoonvarna, climbing the wall of the outdoor toilets to peek at the girls.

Donal leaps up beside me and gets a handhold.

The truck doesn't even notice us. It drives the rest of the way into a dark, confined chamber. The others crowd in around it.

The hatch closes.

We're trapped inside the dome.

Before we have time to panic, air jets into the chamber—it's an airlock—and the other end slides open.

I drop down to the ground and stumble into green-tinged light.

A spear bounces off my helmet.

CHAPTER 10

A spear? No, just a sharpened stick.

I pick it up. More sticks continue to hail down on myself and the others, bouncing harmlessly off our spacesuits. I look around for whoever's throwing them, and spot movement in the trees.

Yes, trees. Big, jungly ones, reaching up to a distant roof that glows a uniform soft white.

"Hey, you!" I shout—pointlessly, as I'm still in my spacesuit. "Come out of there!"

I've got my lightsaber on me, but it's inside my spacesuit. Lacking ready access to it, or any other weapon, I hurl the stick back in the direction it came from.

Boughs dance, leaves fall, and several small stout forms drop to the ground and flee through the undergrowth. Shaggy golden fur, pink naked bottoms. Some kind of monkeys.

"Welcome to the jungle," Donal says. "Well, you do hear of chimpanzees attacking people."

"They must have been waiting for the truck," Harriet says. "We frightened them, poor things."

Meanwhile the dumper truck is rolling away down a road that runs around the inside of the dome. The road is paved with what looks like diamonds.

"I want to know where that's going." I shuffle after the truck as fast as you can in a spacesuit. My mind dances with visions of real live aliens, the last survivors of the Denebite Empire; they've been hiding out here for millennia and will be delighted to see some new faces ... I'll be able to tell them that their great enemies, the Silicon People from the galactic core who invented anti-grav, are no more, and they'll be so happy they shower me with presents ... Admittedly this is farfetched. When the dumper truck turns into a small compound in the jungle, just a couple of hundred yards down the road, I halt and take off my spacesuit. I dig my lightsaber out of my Carhartts.

It's a relief to get out of that horrible articulated balloon, anyway.

The air is fine, as proved by the spear-hurling monkeys, and it feels deliciously cool on my sweaty skin. The smell reminds me of the Fern House at the botanic gardens in Dublin.

"Hurry up, lads," I say to those who've come with me—Donal, Hendrik, the black South African who calls himself Jackal, and Gordon.

They emerge out of their spacesuits into the sound of leaves rustling and water falling nearby. Their expressions of relief and joy give me an idea of what my own face must have looked like when I took my spacesuit off.

Something clanks inside the compound. We sidle through the gateway and see the dumper truck tipping its load of snow into a hopper. That done, it hooks itself up to a charging station.

Otherwise, the compound contains two sheds, empty but for a few dead leaves, and one of those advanced printers the Denebites made, which probably spits out spare parts for the dumper truck when it needs them.

Examining the printer, I get that feeling very strongly, and I can see from Donal's face he's got it, too. What feeling? Why, the feeling you get when an initially promising discovery turns out to be shite. Nothing new here, nothing new.

Gordon says, "It's a wholly automated system. The tipper lorries replenish the water and air supplies, and take out the rubbish. I expect there are other robots around, managing the flora and fauna. It's a Mary Celeste."

Minus the mystery, I think to myself. There's no mystery about the fate of the Denebites. Just like all the other aliens, they're dead, dead, dead.

"I might be able to print out some spare parts for the *Bogtrotter*," Gordon goes on, poking at the printer's Denebite keypad. They counted in base four.

"I thought it was impossible to reprogram those?" Donal says.

"Well, no one's managed it yet," Gordon admits.

"Come on," Donal says, taking him by the elbow. "There's one other thing we didn't find here, apart from aliens, and that's food. Maybe the others have had better luck."

They have.

After stumbling through the forest and calling their names, we find them encamped on the bank of a lake at the bottom of a waterfall. They are picking and eating fruit from the trees around the lake. These fruits include:

- Knobbly pears that taste like dates
- Leaves that taste like sweet 'n' spicy beef jerky
- Nuts that remind me of pecans
- Strawberries the size of your fist

And the water's got an Evian-like flavor.

"This," I say to Imogen, "could be worse."

She grins lazily. "That's Irish for 'I can't believe we got this lucky,' right?"

"Close," I say. "There's got to be a catch."

We're lying on the velvety grass, basking in the light of the roof. It's not so cold that you need your layers, and Imogen has stripped down to a fetching little camisole. The rest of us have lost a shocking amount of weight but she's managed to hang onto her curves. Scratches from fruit-picking stripe her cheeks. Date-pear juice stains her lips brown. I could eat her up.

"Oh, I can think of a few catches," she says. "Such as, we're stuck three and a half kiloparsecs from home, on a planet without a sun, our spaceship's bust, and we'll probably *die* here ..." She giggles.

"Optimism's easier with a full stomach," I agree. I'm playing with a piece of her hair, and she's not stopping me.

"No, but seriously." She props herself on one elbow—removing her hair from my fingers—and gazes at me earnestly. "There's something good about being on an alien planet. I feel different. It was the same on the Burren. I felt like I could finally relax. No pressure to perform. No one watching me."

"Arcadia's an alien planet."

"Oh come on, no it's not. OK, technically. But it's really

just Silicon Valley's outsourcing center. *This* is an alien planet."

I hesitate. "I was going to buy my own planet." It feels risky telling her this. But she seems to feel the same way I do, which is unexpected and amazing. "I'd have named it Fletchworld, or something. It would be all mine."

She doesn't laugh. She doesn't even raise a condescending eyebrow at my common-as-shite dream, shared by many other thousands of men (yes, mostly men). Instead, confusingly, she looks sad. "I get that. I wouldn't have before, but now? I totally get that."

"But recently I've been thinking, a whole planet to myself? It might get a bit lonely."

"No risk of that here," she mutters.

I glance around. Actually, the only people in sight are the three surviving Australians and Gordon, who are sunbathing at a distance. The South Africans have gone hunting, claiming that a vegan diet is not for them, *nee dankie*. Donal and Harriet have gone with them, to prevent them from shooting the monkeys. Kenneth and Vanessa are having it off in the undergrowth. The treecats are chasing birds.

"Imogen …"

"Yes, Fletch?"

The tension in her voice sings like a badly bowed fiddle string. I realize now that it's always there. It was gone for the last few minutes but now it's back.

"Nothing," I say, and lay my lips on hers.

A few minutes later, she pushes me away and carries on talking as if nothing had happened. I hate it when women do that.

"But honestly, I wanted to retire to Treetop someday,"

she says. "And this is kind of like the poor man's version of Treetop, isn't it?"

I am lying on my back, breathing slowly and regularly. "Imogen," I say, "I'm starting to think you are not taking our plight seriously." What I mean is that she's not taking *me* seriously. Or is it the same thing?

"I'm just saying. We could build treehouses."

"Why would we want to?" I say grumpily.

Because that's what they do on Treetop, I suppose. Treetop is an exclusive yuppie planet where everyone lives in treehouses. Donal, I happen to know, had designs on a Treetop condo for himself and Harriet. I'd personally place Treetop in the penultimate circle of suburban hell, next only to Roslevan, the most yuppified suburb of Ennis, where I spent the worst two years of my life working as a assistant caregiver at a nursing home.

"I don't know," she says, and there's a catch in her voice. "I guess I just thought it would make it more homey."

"Ah, Imogen." I sit up and reach for her.

She rolls away from me, wiping the back of one hand across her eyes. With her other hand she slaps at my fondling paw. "Leave me alone! Why are you in such a hurry, anyway? You'll get to screw me sooner or later if we have to stay here!"

She stands up and walks off. I call after her, "Imogen!" but she doesn't turn around, and I get the feeling it would not be a good idea to go after her.

Left alone, puzzled and frustrated, I stare at the bubbles floating on the lake. It's like the flipping Garden of Eden here. Well, it may have been until we arrived. The treecats have caught a bird and are ripping into its gorgeously plumed carcase.

Could we do it?

I mentally add us up. Me, Imogen, Donal, Harriet, Kenneth, Vanessa, Gordon, Hendrik, Shaka, Jackal, Adriaan, and by a stroke of fate all three of the surviving Australians are women. Fifteen of us, split almost equally between the sexes. We've got stacker expertise in the form of Gordon, and tech resources in the form of the *Intergalactic Bogtrotter*—she may not fly anymore, but she could be dismantled for parts. Barring unforeseen drawbacks, we *could* do it.

And it doesn't seem such a bad way for my adventuring to end.

Sorry, Finian, I tried. At least I've lived up to your low expectations of me, right?

Imogen's walking along the lakeshore. She's left her sweatshirt behind. I pick it up. I'll take it to her. A pretext to ask her why she walked off.

We *could* do it, I'll tell her. And I'll find some non-awful way to make it clear that she doesn't have to sleep with me if she doesn't want to.

She's charging back towards me, arms pumping. "Give me that!" she shouts as she gets in range.

"This?"

The sweatshirt crackles.

I open the zippered kangaroo pocket as she snatches at it.

MRE wrappers float out. Jesus, there are dozens of them, all folded up small. I unfold one and read, "Pork Chow Mein."

Red to the ears, Imogen scrabbles up the evidence.

"It was *you* who filched those, Imogen," I say. "And you

let Kenneth take the blame."

"It was the treecats."

"It was not the fecking treecats! It was you."

"I *fed* them to the treecats! I didn't eat them myself!"

"Looks like you ate some of them," I say, rudely aiming a swat at her bottom.

"Ask Harriet if you don't believe me!"

"That's just as bad, anyway! The point is you lied about it, and two men are dead as a result."

"Oh, I bet you really miss Armando. Anyway, I saw you push him. Kenneth stabbed him because he thought he shoved him, but it was you."

"Imogen," I say with distant, false politeness, "I don't remember if I've ever asked you. Why did you get fired from Samsung?"

It was Samsung that brought her out to Arcadia to work as a reverse-engineer. But then they let her go, after which she began her downhill slide from taxi driver, to sales rep, to working for us.

"They fired me for not being a team player," she admits.

I laugh mirthlessly. "You don't say."

Harriet's incomparable bullhorn of a voice comes from the forest. "Hey everyone! Wakey wakey!"

The hunting party tramps out of the trees. They have not got any game. What they *have* got is a dozen of the spear-hurling monkeys. These are walking with them—Harriet's got two of them by the hands—and it's obvious their bodies are built for walking upright, after all. They are not, in fact, monkeys. With their chubby furred bodies, white tummies, and black button eyes and noses, they look more like …

"Ewoks!" Imogen whispers, entranced.

"Sssh," I say. "Star Wars is a sensitive subject around here." I've got one hand on my lightsaber in case the little fellas turn nasty again, although they're acting like well-behaved schoolchildren now.

"How do you mean?"

"We used to have a wookie on the crew." Poor Woolly; the Butterfly-zillas killed her. Of course she wasn't really a wookie. None of that sort are. It's just cosplay taken to extremes.

But these little fellas are not cosplaying. They're live aliens and they're twittering at us in growly little voices that remind me of … "Care Bears," I say out loud.

"Care Bears?" says Imogen, who is Canadian, after all.

Donal laughs. "He used to have a robot one when we were little. It *did* sound like that, didn't it, Fletch?"

"Thanks for ruining my image," I say to Donal, mock-angry, and add to Imogen in an undertone: "Don't worry. Ewoks are only Care Bears that lost their homes in a forest fire, anyway."

She cracks up as if she's never heard that one before. I amble over to get a better look at the Care Bears of the Lost Planet. They've charmed our dour South Africans properly. Hendrik says: "They saw us throwing sticks at squirrels, and came to say, 'You are doing it wrong.'"

"Did they actually *say* that?"

"No, but they use sign language." He's gleeful. "They want to give us spear-throwing lessons!"

It's clear to me that the Care Bears of the Lost Planet are not *saying* anything. They're just growling and waving their paws.

"They're intelligent!" Harriet says giddily.

Oh Jesus, not this again.

I remind everyone that this is exactly what we went through with the treecats. Harriet thought they were intelligent at first, only to be disappointed in the end.

But no one's interested in my opinion. A few spear-throwing lessons and a shared meal of roast squirrel later, they're all convinced that we have discovered the first ever race of *living* sapient aliens. Gordon is recording their voices on his iPhone and running them through various pieces of software to look for linguistic patterns. The clinching piece of evidence for him was that the Care Bears of the Lost Planet know how to start fires (the Boy Scout method) and what's more, they know how to do it *safely*, in a dome filled with trees. He also points out that they wear ornaments—little silvery rocks with holes through, strung on dried vines.

One unexpected ally shares my skepticism about the CB of the LPs' sapience.

"Fletch?" says Kenneth. "I have a confession to make."

"Do I look like a priest?"

"Not that kind of confession."

"OK."

"I wasn't the pilot of the *Hellraiser.*"

"Erm, we already agreed on that."

"I wasn't the cook, either."

"I didn't think you were. What were you really, then? Second assistant bootlicker to the Cannibal Captain?"

"I was the xenobiologist."

"The *Hellraiser* had a xenobiologist?"

"Yeah, well, I was really just cover for when people would

ask 'Why does an exploration ship need so many guns?' It sucked."

"OK. And?"

"Those little guys aren't sapient."

"That's in your expert opinion?"

"Fuck off. I may not have gone to Harvard, but I am qualified in my field, OK?"

"I believe you, I believe you. I'm just wondering what you're basing that on."

"Oh, people thought dolphins and whales were sapient for ages. Billions of dollars were wasted trying to communicate with them. It turns out they're only about as smart as elephants. Yes, they have a limited faculty for language, but that doesn't make them sapient. Chimpanzees use tools. That doesn't make them sapient, either. The test is, are they *learning* any faster than they're *evolving?* And the answer is no. These little guys have been stuck in here for millions of years, right?" Kenneth spreads his hands as if to say, there's your answer.

"Tell Harriet what you just told me," I suggest.

He shudders.

"Well, she'll figure it out eventually," I say. "They all will."

And in the meantime, what's the harm? It's like Imogen dreaming of building a tree house. We all need something to distract ourselves from the fact that we're probably stuck here forever.

Humans of the Lost Planet.

Maybe a million years from now, our descendants will have evolved to have fur, and hunt squirrels with sharpened sticks.

CHAPTER 11

But all good things must come to an end, and our romance with the Care Bears of the Lost Planet ends abruptly when they get into it with the treecats.

One minute all our alien friends are lazing happily by the lake, the next minute the fur is flying.

Harriet gets badly scratched trying to pull them apart. The whole heap of them brawl off into the woods. We track them down to the tree that the treecats, true to their nature, have colonized, and discover that Fluffington, Chairman Meow, and friends have lined their nests with silvery gravel, each piece with a hole in it.

The little kleptos have raided the CB of the LPs' village for sparklies.

This is my first visit to the Care Bears' village, which Harriet, Gordon, and Vanessa have been raving about for days. It *does* look like it might have been built by creatures about as smart as, oh, honeybees. Leafy-roofed shacks *(not treehouses)* cluster around the roots of a forest giant the size of a California redwood. There are A-frames where they dry the beef-jerky leaves to make them even more like beef jerky, I suppose. At the sight of all the baby CBs tumbling around, even my stony heart melts a little.

The most amazing thing is it doesn't stink. I have visited more than one 'developing colony,' and the thing that always sticks out is the lack of plumbing. I don't know where the Care Bears of the Lost Planet bury their poop, but they clearly don't shit where they live. This puts them streets ahead of humanity on at least one count.

They have little silver jingles hanging over the doors of their shacks, similar to the ornaments they wear around their necks. Out of nowhere Fluffington swarms up a doorpost and swipes a pawful of these. The baby CBs squeal in terror.

"We're wrecking this place," Kenneth says, stricken.

I can see what he means, as the treecats and Care Bears mix it up again. We're worse than the idjits who introduced rabbits to Australia.

I wander away from the melee and find Gordon sitting on a tree root, tossing a bubble from hand to hand.

The dome is full of these mysterious objects. We've stopped noticing them except to kick them out of the way. We tried to have a game of football at one point, but they're too light. They work better for water polo.

"Fivebranes," Gordon greets me.

"Huh?" I start to sit down, and spring back as a spindly metal biped stalks around the tree. It's one of the Denebite maintenance robots Gordon predicted. Their main job is to gather up the bubbles, which is what this one's doing now—there are loads of them trapped in the tree roots.

"They must be fivebranes," Gordon mutters.

"What're fivebranes?"

"Five-dimensional membranes. I'm sorry, I know this isn't

your wheelhouse. Essentially, these bubbles are spherical force fields. Solid objects can pass through them, but air can't. Nor can electromagnetic waves. I assume that's due to the quantum properties of objects with both electric and magnetic charge …"

He rambles on in this vein but I am not listening anymore. *"Force fields!?!"*

That's only item number four, or maybe three, on the big backers' A-tech wish lists. Imagine a spaceship made of force fields. You wouldn't even need a hull! Imagine orbital habitats with transparent walls and floors! Imagine, imagine … imagine me claiming this discovery and auctioning off the patent to the tune of billions …

I grip Gordon's arm. "We've got to get off this planet!"

"Well, yes."

"These things would go for billions!"

"Perhaps, perhaps, but they're not reverse-engineerable."

The maintenance robot stalks towards us. Gordon offers it the bubble—the *force field*—he is holding. The robot delicately takes it and puts it into its net sack. "You're welcome," Gordon says dryly to the machine.

"Do they even know we're here? The robots."

"In a sense, I imagine. We're furniture."

"I've been called worse things." I freeze. "Hang on, how do you know these force fields aren't reverse-engineerable?"

"Because we tried."

At last it dawns on me. "This is it, isn't it? Finian's stunning discovery."

"Yes."

"But you'd never been here before. You didn't know this planet existed."

"No," Gordon says, and I suddenly remember him on the first day we got here, kicking the bubbles outside the dome and shouting in an uncharacteristic spasm of rage: *Oh bloody hell,* or something like that. "It was quite a surprise," he says now. "We'd no idea where the things came from. We found several thousand of them on Omega Centauri 49, the planet I mentioned to you. There's nothing particularly interesting about 49. Most of it looks like Wales, with a few Denebite ruins scattered around. Our only discovery of note was the force fields, which clearly merited study. But we had made no progress with them before Special Delivery Sam attacked us."

"Far be it from me to question your expertise, Gordon. But the reverse-engineers on Arcadia are fairly good at what they do—"

Gordon doesn't like this. "I assure you, we ran all the same tests they would. The *Marauding Elephant* has a first-class lab. *Had,*" he sighs. "Well, now we know where the things came from. *Here.*" We can still hear the noise of brawling Care Bears and treecats in the distance. "As I originally theorized, this planet must have been ripped away from its sun. The Denebites kept it going by building these domes and herding the Care Bears inside." It's funny to hear him unselfconsciously utter the words *Care Bears.* "But *why?* What makes the Care Bears so all-fired important? And where are the force fields manufactured? Maybe they're just decorations. No one knows how the Denebites thought, the poxy duck-faced busybodies."

Decorations. That sparks a connection. "The silvery ornaments the Care Bears wear, could they be—"

"Oh yes, undoubtedly." Gordon looks around for a

bubble. The robot has picked up all the ones nearby. Suddenly one falls out of the branches over our heads. "Perhaps there's a factory in the roof," Gordon grumps. "Anyway, look at this." He picks the bubble up. "May I borrow your lightsaber?"

I reluctantly hand it over.

Gordon sets the beam to 'short' and stabs the bubble. The bright blue beam bursts it like a balloon. For a second it smells like somebody farted. Then Gordon's hand is covered in silvery clingfilm, and he's laughing, dropping the lightsaber, balling the stuff up. "You've got about thirty seconds to work it before it hardens."

I snatch the ex-bubble from him and stretch it like silly putty.

"Ordinary lasers won't pop them. Only the lightsabers. Finian made that discovery. No doubt Special Delivery Sam is still shooting and microwaving the things, getting increasingly frustrated." Gordon cackles.

"Hang on, you said solid objects go through them?"

"Yes, if they're moving fast enough."

"But energy doesn't?"

"No, not unless it's the particular wavelength used by the lightsabers."

"Then why don't we use them to mend the *Intergalactic Bogtrotter?*"

Gordon stares at me. "Occasionally," he says, "you have rather good ideas."

CHAPTER 12

A couple of hours later we're all out on the surface of the Lost Planet, sticking force fields over the holes in the *Bogtrotter's* reactor turbine vessels and heat exchanger pipes as fast as I can deflate them with my lightsaber. Gordon keeps saying, "I think this is going to work! I think it's actually going to work!" A frenzy possesses us. Not even I knew how badly I wanted to leave the Lost Planet until I realized that it might, after all, be possible.

At last Gordon says he's ready to try bootstrapping the reactor. Donal and I head for the bridge. Because the *Bogtrotter* landed badly, with one wing buried in the snow, all the floors are tilted at a steep gradient. We pass the three Australian girls chipping their dead colleagues out of the ice deposits in the mess. Donal, being a good captain, stops to be compassionate. I carry on to the bridge and find Imogen on her knees, poking around inside that safe of hers.

"What are you doing?"

"Fuck off!"

I sense a certain froideur. She hasn't forgiven me for uncovering her MRE theft, even though I didn't tell anyone.

"Sure, excuse me for breathing," I mutter, and shuffle past her to boot up the various screens and displays.

The first instrument that comes alive is the multidirectional radar.

"Oi, what's that?"

Imogen flies to my side. "What?"

The radar's set up to track our sats in orbit. Obviously, we didn't drop any sats in orbit. Yet there is something up there all the same.

ESTIMATED ORBITAL ALTITUDE: 13,500 MILES
ORBIT TYPE: GEOSTATIONARY

"What the feck is that?!" Donal shoves me aside.

"It's a ship, dimwit," I say. And because Donal has a tendency to be hopeful when things are bleakest, I add: "Special Delivery Sam's found us."

After all, they'd have known where we came off the Railroad. It was the same place where they attacked us. All they had to do was come off the Railroad themselves and sniff around a bit.

"I don't think it can be them," Imogen says, her voice thin. "I mean, why are they just sitting up there?"

"Donal!" Harriet shouts over the radio. She always forgets that with suit-to-suit radios, you don't have to shout. I clap my gloves pointlessly to my helmet. "We've got COMPANY!"

"Guess they're not just sitting up there, after all," I smile at Imogen, and bolt off the bridge.

We squeeze out through one of the still-unmended holes in the fuselage. The icy plain stretches bleak all around our poor, crippled ship. Harriet points up.

A shooting star. It's getting brighter and brighter. It's a

ship de-orbiting. The same one we saw, or their friends? Who cares? There's another—there are *three* of them, and they're coming in right on top of us!

We stumble back to the dome, strung out across the plain. When we came out, following one of the dumper trucks, we wedged this end of the airlock open with a tree branch. Thank God, the branch is still in place. We crowd inside.

It is at this point that I first question our unthinking herd instinct to run for safety. "Leave the branch there for a second, Donal!" I stand athwart it, peering through the man-width gap.

Three bombs go off on the plain, at least that's what it looks like. Vacuum or no vacuum, I can *feel* the incredible noise of the thrusters in my bones. When the smoke and the fountaining snow clears away, three ships stand dangerously near the *Intergalactic Bogtrotter.*

They are, as I expected, up-armored DC-100s with *Sam-I-Am* painted on their fuselages.

Your man must have stolen a whole fleet of the things.

Almost before the thruster shields have stopped glowing red, people swarm down the steps of the DC-100s. They wear a motley variety of spacesuits, everything from marshmallows to sleek A-tech suits. I can see their guns from here, wicked sticks over their shoulders. They swarm around the *Intergalactic Bogtrotter,* besieging the wallies they imagine to be in there.

At the same time, others are discovering the force field bubbles littering the plain.

"Fletch, come on!" Donal begs.

The diamond-stuff the dome is made of blocks radio frequencies. I lean a bit further out, so I can get a signal, and fiddle with the wrist controls on my EVA suit until I pick up someone bellowing, "Oh my freaking God! There are millions of them!"

Maybe they'll just load up on force fields and go away?

No sooner have I had this hopeful thought than a fountain of snow kicks up in my face. Some bastard with a long-range scope's spotted me!

"There they are!" he, or one of his friends, yells.

Donal grabs the back of my spacesuit, yanks me inside, and kicks the branch away. The airlock slams shut.

We spill into the forest. Everyone pulls off their helmets, yammering. A group of CBs of the LP look on from the trees.

"Quiet, QUIET!" Donal's got a voice on him too, when he sees fit to use it. "First of all, are you shot, Fletch?"

"Amn't," I say grumpily. "They've got horrible aim."

"Right, everyone CALM DOWN! They can't get in for another …" Donal looks at his watch. "Six hours. That's how long it is until the truck goes out again. Until then, they'll be cooling their heels outside, same as we were when we first got here. So we've got time to plan our counter-attack."

Brave words.

But when he and I are alone, sitting in the crutch of the big tree facing the airlock, Donal confesses that he hasn't got a plan. "Apart from hiding until they go away."

I stare at the airlock. We can hear them banging on the outside of the dome. They can't break in ahead of schedule. No one can defeat Denebite automation … but in another five hours and five minutes, Denebite automation will open up the front door for them.

"We *could* hide until they go away," I say slowly. "This place is fecking huge. There's no way they've got the manpower to search it properly. But …"

"If they give up and go away, there goes our only chance of getting home," Donal quietly acknowledges.

I nod. They've got the *Bogtrotter,* and if they can't fly it away, it is a sure bet that they will blow it up for sheer spite. So much for Gordon's hours of patient work.

"Our best chance," Donal says, "and it's probably our only chance, is to capture one of their ships."

I stare at him, glad we're alone. "Seriously, Donal? Capture one of their ships? With *this* crew?"

Donal's face grows whiter. He doesn't have any real grasp of the possible. That's why he is an explorer and not a pirate. I hate myself for dragging him into this.

"You got any better ideas?" he says truculently.

"Erm. No."

He stares at me. I do a big shrug: *sorry.*

And then he bursts out laughing, this pal of mine, who's never held anything against me, even when we got caught shoplifting from Dunnes Stores and I lied to the guards that it was his idea. "Yeah, well we'll just have to give it a go then, won't we?" he says.

I will get him and the others safely off this planet if it kills me. He and Harriet *will* have their Treetop condo.

"Well," I say, "we *might* be able to pull it off. But it's going to take everyone doing as they're told, no messing about …"

The growly squeals of Care Bears interrupt our discussion. We crane out of the tree. Three full-grown CBs are running full tilt down the road from the charging station. One is a female, with an infant clinging to her chest fur. The other two are males, carrying forcefield bubbles in their paws.

A maintenance robot stalks after them, gaining ground.

"It's *chasing* them!" Donal says.

The Care Bears sprint under our tree. The female trips over the big branch we left lying there. She rolls like a furry ball, ending up on her back with baby on her chest.

The maintenance robot catches up with a spidery leap.

A laser beam lances out of its thorax, exactly the same shade of blue as my lightsaber's beam.

The two male Care Bears thrust their forcefield bubbles into the beam …

… as it bores into the helpless infant.

"Aw feck!"

With a cry of disgust, I leap out of the tree and slash the maintenance robot in half with my lightsaber.

"Baby-killer!" I shout at the robot's twitching halves.

"So you *do* believe they're sapient," Harriet says sadly behind me.

The infant is dead. Its mother keens over its body. The males press close to her, shaping their now-deflated bubbles into silvery ornaments, which they lay on the poor little corpse.

"Bloody hell," I say. "They're making those in the baby's memory." I am shaken; would dolphins do this? Elephants build graveyards …

"I gather this is the first time you've seen a cull," Harriet says. "It's a population-control measure, I assume. All fully automated. The Care Bears have no way to resist. But as you can see for yourself, they've developed ways to memorialize their dead."

All those ornaments hanging at the doors of their shacks stand for dead babies. No wonder they were upset when the treecats stole them.

"King Herod's got nothing on the bloody Denebites," Donal says. Suddenly he explodes, "I hate this fecking place!"

The male Care Bears are pawing at the bisected maintenance robot, as if wondering will it come back to life. They glance at my lightsaber with a hopeful surmise.

Donal's right. This isn't the Garden of Eden. It's a Denebite zoo, or maybe a jail. I could destroy all the maintenance robots, but then the dome would break down. There are a thousand other tasks they do that keep the place running.

Harriet slides her hand into Donal's. "Have you thought of a plan?" she says, wincing at another bang on the outside of the dome.

Donal takes a deep breath. "Well, sort of …"

CHAPTER 13

Time for action.

The dumper truck trundles down the road from its parking garage and noses up to the airlock.

Donal and I are sat high up in the same tree as before, hidden from the ground by the abundant leaves. The others are scattered in other trees nearby. We killed time by going for one last swim and collecting as much fruit as we could carry.

The dumper truck rolls silently into the airlock chamber. It closes.

The bashing on the outside of the dome stops.

The dumper truck usually spends fifteen to twenty minutes outside. We stare at our watches.

Again the airlock opens.

Twenty, twenty-one, twenty-two individuals in red-and-navy-blue spacesuits leap out of the dumper truck's skip and stare around wildly.

These must be Special Delivery Sam's elite troops. They grab some of the force field bubbles that are lying around, throw them at each other, and exclaim in American accents.

Donal and I shake with silent hilarity. It's like watching a replay of our own arrival, minus the spear-hurling Care Bears. I could take out a few of them here and now if I wasn't dying of laughter.

But they're armed with laser carbines and shotguns and fairly soon they calm down. A tall, curly-headed fella gives orders. "OK, let's split up … Annika, Jesse, you guys hang out here. Everyone else pair off and search the dome. Those goddamn punks must be here somewhere."

"Is that Special Delivery Sam?" Donal whispers into my ear.

"No clue."

"Have you never seen a picture of him?"

"No. But that can't be him, can it? He's supposed to be at least Finian's age."

"He's probably leading from the back," Donal whispers.

The Samites jog under our tree and scatter into the forest.

They've left their spacesuits lying in a heap in front of the airlock.

I nudge Donal and point.

He nods, his face bright with hope.

Jesse, a rangy black lad, and Annika, who looks as Swedish as her name, sit down on the spacesuits. They chat a bit, speculating if the airlock will ever reopen, or if they're stuck in here forever—it's déjà vu all over again, honestly. I feel like shouting down to them, 'Don't worry, the truck will be back in twelve hours and seven minutes,' but our plan, such as it is, depends on the fact that they don't yet know the timing of the truck's runs.

Annika wraps some force field bubbles in a spacesuit for a pillow, and curls up for a nap. Jesse lights a cigarette.

The smoke curls up to us. It makes me crave one. Jesus, I gave up the fags fifteen years ago.

But it's purgatory sitting in this tree, not making a sound, not daring to move, *with* our fecking spacesuits on, all but the helmets …

… for another *twelve* hours.

Six hours into our wait, Donal drops off to sleep, the jammy bastard.

Jesse and Annika exchange radio updates with their friends. I earwig. The other Samites have discovered the Care Bears of the Lost Planet. The CBs of the LP have thrown spears at them and run away, surprise, surprise. Now the Samites have shelved their search for us, and are in full cry after the CBs. I hope they don't find the village.

T minus 4 hours 37 minutes. This is worse than a transatlantic flight. I occupy myself by coming up with exercises to pass the time.

- Flex legs (careful not to dislodge any leaves or twigs!)
- Scratch inside spacesuit
- Undo spacesuit seals to scratch the really itchy places
- Take spacesuit off (leaves and twigs!)
  Ah God that's better.
- Make top ten list of best rock albums
- Top ten actresses I would like to sleep with
- Top ten places I wish I was now (all of them are far far away from Omega fecking Centauri)
- Top ten candidates for the name of my planet when I finally get it

I have to abandon that exercise partway through. It's too depressing. It seems so very, very unlikely that I will ever have my own planet now.

More radio updates provide a welcome distraction. The Samites found our camp by the lake, and some of those bloody MRE packets. "Stay alert," says the leader over the radio. "This Connolly's a crazy fucker. Runs in the family, I guess."

Ha ha ha from Jesse and Annika, although I don't see what's so funny.

♦ Pray

30 seconds later:

"Donal. Wake up."

"Mmph," Donal says.

I clap my hand over his mouth.

Something moves in the canopy above us.

The furry face of a CB pokes down through the leaves.

Ah, the poor wee thing's been stuck up here with us all this time, scared to go down the tree …

The CB turns around, showing us its naked pink bottom. It grunts.

Jesse and Annika are on their feet, staring up. I pray they can't see us through the leaves.

The CB's anus stretches. A glint of silver emerges.

I stare, gobsmacked, as the CB shits a fully formed force field bubble onto Donal's head.

So *that's* where they come from.

"Ah Jesus," Donal's awake, wiping his face. The new bubble must have been sticky.

"They're Care Bear poop!" I whisper. *"That's* why there's always thousands of them lying around!"

The bubble drifts down to the ground.

Jesse shoots it.

I am charmed to see that it continues on its drifting

course, unaffected by shotgun pellets. Gordon was right: solid objects do go through them if they're moving fast enough.

"Another lovely, lovely force field," Annika says, running after it.

Jesse laughs in embarrassment. "Why're there so many of them around here, anyway?" he wonders aloud.

Ah my lad, I think, if only you knew. We were swimming with them, playing football with them ... we mended our *ship* with Care Bear poop. That's disgusting!

Donal is cracking up as the truth sinks in.

"T minus twelve minutes," I whisper to him. "Get ready."

We daren't use the radios to alert the others. We just have to hope they're watching the time, too.

T minus eight minutes, and the curly-headed leader of the Samites strolls out of the trees, eating a date-pear.

The luck of the Irish strikes again.

Donal curses under his breath. I whisper, "Don't panic! Don't panic! We can take them all!"

"They're just kids!"

Yes, and I have sat up here for twelve hours hearing about the vintage Gibson guitar Jesse wants to buy, and Annika's boyfriend troubles, but— "I'll do it, OK? I will do it!"

"So what's the deal, Sam?" Jesse says. "You figure we're stuck in here?"

THIS is Special Delivery Sam?

"Meh," says curly-head. "That truck went out once, it's gotta go out again."

T minus six minutes.

There's no time like the present.

I slide down the tree at the speed of sound. Glad I took

off my spacesuit. What I lose in protection I gain in mobility. I've got my lightsaber in my bare right hand. Halfway down the tree, I slash the beam across the clearing on maximum range setting, catching Annika in the leg, oh Jesus I'm sorry, love, and Jesse is shooting up at me and I slash at him. The beam takes the side of his head off. I hit the ground screaming for him, because he can't scream anymore.

"Fuuuck," Sam says, staring at the bodies of his friends. He belatedly connects me with the carnage. His gun starts to come up.

"Don't move," I say, swaying. My lightsaber scribbles gouges in the dirt at his feet.

He drops the gun. He's got a brain on him, this one.

"You are my prisoner, is that fecking clear, arsehole?" I snap.

Donal slides down the tree. The others come running out of their hiding places. Harriet screams. Someone else breaks into sobs. Through all this I hear the heavenly noise of the dumper truck's tires squelching on the road.

Sam's eyes dart all over the place, then fasten on me again. "I was supposed to make sure you were dead," he says.

I shrug. If I open my mouth, I'll puke. I can't believe I killed them.

"My dad is gonna murder me," Sam says. "I guess Finian was wrong, huh?"

"Wait." I can speak without puking, after all. "What did Finian say?"

"Oh, he said you were crap in a fight." Sam laughs morosely.

I'll fecking show him, I think, and then— "Hang on, he's alive?"

"He also said you were a total douche." Sam rolls his eyes. "It's like, thanks, oh legendary piratical one. Now he's got my mom convinced this Fletcher Connolly character is a threat to her entire empire. So I blow you off the Railroad, but that's not good enough, so I have to chase down the wreckage of your ship and grind it into infinitely small pieces of interstellar debris ..." He says this last part in a sing-song, and I realize he's mimicking his mother. I always assumed Special Delivery Sam was a man, but evidently she's a woman. And this is her son. "So I come all the way out here to finish the job, and now you've SHOT two of my FRIENDS!"

The dumper truck rolls into the clearing, straight over Annika.

Sam Junior winces. *"But,"* he says, "I'm willing to overlook that. You found the force fields, right? I can't believe how many of them are just lying around here. Those things are freaking *currency,* man. So here's my plan. We grab as many of them as my ships will carry and light out for Arcadia. What do you say?"

"Whisht!"

"Yeah, I know they can't be reverse-engineered. But imagine how much they'd go for per piece."

This lad's talking my language, I think for a fleeting instant, and then Donal yells, "Fletch, come on!"

The truck's inside the airlock. Donal's jammed this end with the same old branch wedged crosswise. The others are changing into the spacesuits left behind by Sam's party. Sam watches this operation with mounting horror.

"Oh yeah," I say to him, "and you can't use your radio to communicate with anyone outside the dome. But I expect you've already found that out."

I squeeze into one of their spacesuits. Gordon covers Sam with my lightsaber while I'm doing up the seals. Donal's begging Harriet to leave the treecats.

"The whats?" Sam says, looking at the cat carriers that, I now observe, the girls are loading into the dumper truck.

Everyone doing what they're told.

No messing about.

Oh sure, that'll be no problem, says Donal, ever-optimistic.

"We are NOT taking the FECKING treecats!" I roar. I jump into the truck and hurl the cat carriers out.

And I'm not quite sure what happens next because it starts with Harriet punching me in the groin, and these spacesuits of Sam's, being fancy A-tech ones, have nothing to cushion the blow.

Sprawled on the truck bed, blinking through tears of pain, I see blurry shapes leaping over me. There's a melee in the entrance of the airlock, some trying to get out, others trying to pull them back.

I never see who kicks the branch away.

But I'm pretty sure that one of the South Africans—Adriaan, the quiet fella, who's always showing you pics of his kids—did it on purpose.

The airlock slams shut.

"You asshole," Imogen hisses in the dark, to me, I assume.

A quick roll call confirms that we've lost Harriet, Vanessa, Jasmine (one of the Australian women), and Donal.

CHAPTER 14

The dumper truck rolls out onto the plain. According to its ponderous habit of many millennia, it tilts up its skip and tips us out.

I'm still reeling from the shock of losing Donal and the three women. Not to mention the agonizing effects of Harriet's right hook.

We can't go on with the plan. But we *are* going on with the plan, whether I want to or not. There were dozens of people gathering up bubbles when we emerged, and now they're all around us, wanting to know what we found inside the dome, "Did you waste 'em, Sam?" and "Where are the others?" because if we were Sam's raiding party there should be twice as many of us.

I know I'll give the game away as soon as I open my mouth. It was supposed to be Donal who handled this part. He's got the gift of the gab and he can do a wicked American accent.

Hopelessly, I say, "Well, guys, I'll give you the good news first. There are millions of force field bubbles lying around here, as you've discovered, and those things are freaking *currency,* man …"

Oh Jesus, I sound like a jackeen trying to talk gangsta.

A hulking Samite picks me up and shakes me. "Say what, asshole? Who the fack is you, anyways?"

Kenneth pipes up. "Hey, is that Doug the Shiv?"

Consternation among the Samites.

"Who's that? Where's Sam?"

"In there," says Kenneth, the traitor, the survivor off the *Hellraiser* who we kept around knowing full well that he used to be a pirate. Thinking, wrongly, that he'd been scared straight. Believing in his ramen-eating, crap-music-loving, double-digit-IQ persona. Feeling *sorry* for him.

This was only supposed to be an exploration trip.

And maybe it would have been, maybe we would've been halfway back to Arcadia by now, if Kenneth hadn't betrayed us to Special Delivery Sam. I see it plainly, too late. These arseholes all talk to each other on their private subreddits.

"It's Ken the Xenobiologist!"

"Dang, man, how'd you get here?"

I writhe, trying to break loose from the enormous Samite who rejoices in the name of Doug the Shiv.

"I ast you who the fack is you?" says D the S.

"Oh," Kenneth says, "ignore him. He's a douche."

Ignore, it turns out, is pirate for *kick the daylights out of.*

Waking, groaning, in solid darkness, the first thing I notice is I'm spacesuit-less again. The second thing is that Doug the Shiv must have practised his goal kicks on me extensively while I was out.

It hurts to move my *toes.*

I can hear a familiar combination of background noises—humming, rumbling, banging. I'm on board a ship.

Moaning in pain, I explore the darkness by touch. I'm in a two-bunker cabin. There's one person in the top bunk, me in the bottom bunk, and three on the floor.

It's like being back on the *Skint Idjit,* without the party atmosphere.

With some difficulty I wake the others up. They turn out to be Shaka, Adriaan, Gail (another of the Australian women) and Gordon.

Not having much to lose at this point, we shout and kick the door—actually, Shaka and Gail kick it. I hurt too much. But nothing happens, and nothing happens, and even Shaka is at the giving-up stage when the door finally opens.

Kenneth's scrawny form blocks out the light.

Shaka growls and seizes him by the neck.

"Lemme go! Ow! *OW!*"

"Out of my way," I say, trying to squeeze past them.

"Mmmph-uggh!" Kenneth pushes something at me.

My lightsaber.

"Let him go, Shaka!"

It's amazing how one little piece of A-tech can improve your day.

I glance up and down the dimly lit corridor, getting my bearings. Now I know where we are. There's not much room on a converted DC-100. The crew all have to sleep in titchy cabins off this corridor at the back of the ship, above the engineering deck.

"I'm goddamn freeing you, if you noticed," Kenneth croaks.

"Yeah, thanks, Kenneth."

"I know Sam from way back. I *could* have just switched sides and left you to rot. But I actually got to like you guys."

"I said thank you, Kenneth."

"I don't want to work for Special Delivery. She's the worst employer in the business. I probably would have ended up digging potatoes on Omega Centauri 49. It's like Wales, only the weather is worse."

I move down the corridor towards the back of the ship, rapping my knuckles on the doors. I can't hear if anyone's in there because Kenneth's still telling us what a hero he is.

"And Vanessa's stuck in the dome! They were saying we should just leave them! So I'm like, no, man. This is *not* going to happen. But I have zero pull around here. So I thought, OK, if anyone can handle this, Fletch can …"

This is what comes of murdering innocent pirates. Now I've got a reputation to live down to. I use my lightsaber to burn through the keypad locks on the cabin doors.

Out come Hendrik, Adriaan, Florence (the third Australian), Jackal, and Imogen—who shrugs me off when I try to hug her.

Out come several people I recall from our muster on the Burren.

Out comes Ruby, his make-up smeared all over his face.

And out come Padraig and Milton and Big Colm off the *Marauding Elephant* …

… and Finian himself.

He's been badly used. He's got a black eye, and he's shirtless, his once-white chest hair matted with blood. I hope it's someone else's. He stares at me expressionlessly.

"I'm freeing you," I point out. Now I know how Kenneth felt.

"Aye, thanks, lad."

And then he's hurtling towards the other end of the

corridor, roaring, "Old Elephants! With me! Men! Women! We can TAKE this fecking ship! Show the pirates no more mercy than they showed us on the Burren!"

Nearly all the freed prisoners surge after him, howling.

Stop them? I might as well try to stop a wave at a football stadium.

And if you thought what happened on the bridge of the *Intergalactic Bogtrotter* was stomach-turning, I will spare you the details of what happens when Finian storms the bridge of the *Bagged & Tagged*. It's inhuman, man—as Hendrik might say, and if he ever has the nerve to say that again, I will remind him how he cut the head off Doug the Shiv and drop-kicked it across the mess. He was a well-brought-up Afrikaaner boy, private school and everything, and then he went on the Railroad. It's desperate what this life can do to you.

It's begun doing it to me, too. I killed those two kids in the dome. I still can't quite believe I did that, and I refuse to kill any more, especially when others are so enthusiastically doing it for me.

I loiter in the rear, flourishing my lightsaber from time to time in case anyone's watching. When the chaos dies down, I scrounge around for a spacesuit that hasn't got a dead body inside it.

Finian's on the bridge. He's swivelled the gun turrets to cover Sam's other two ships. Bellowing abuse over the radio, he waves an AR-15 at the terrified survivors of the *Bagged & Tagged*. "Where are you going?" he says when he sees me all suited up.

"Back into the dome. Donal's in there. Give me twelve hours, a bit more."

"What dome?"

"That one."

He zooms the viewscreen, only now noticing that the Lost Planet has features other than the two remaining Samite ships. "That's alien shite."

"It is."

"Bugger the domes. This planet's covered in gold. The hold of this ship's half filled with force fields already. Do you know what force fields are? They're fecking brilliant. Best A-tech material ever." He holds up his lightsaber, and winks. "You've just got to have one of these to make the most of them."

"We did actually figure that out, Finian," Gordon says, behind me. "We were patching the *Bogtrotter* with them when you came along."

Finian laughs. "You're not a stacker for nothing."

"It was Fletch's idea, actually."

I look around, surprised to get credit from this source. Gordon's in his Old Elephant suit, tusked helmet in his hand.

"Right, right," Finian says, focusing on his enemies once more. "Come out of there with your hands up, or I'll blow you to feck! Now what were you saying, Fletch?"

I have had enough. "See you later," I say, and stomp off the bridge as fast as my aching ribs will allow. Kenneth joins me in the airlock. He's the only other one coming. The rest of our lot are either wounded, or not interested in anything except getting off the Lost Planet as fast as possible.

It's an evil feeling walking across the snow under the guns of the DC-100s. All three are locked down, their railgun turrets trained on one another. Finian's already won this thing, but the lads in the other ships don't know it yet.

I refuse to look back to see if they're targeting me. I trudge past the poor old *Intergalactic Bogtrotter*. Kenneth's far ahead of me, running to catch the truck.

I nearly jump out of my skin when two of the Old Elephants catch up with me.

Gordon.

And Finian.

"You should have told me Donal's trapped in there," my uncle says.

"I did. You weren't listening."

"I've known him since he was wee. He's a solid lad."

Whereas I'm a douche who is crap in a fight, I suppose. But I've only Sam's word for it Finian said that. In reality it was probably 'useless gowl' or something like that.

."He takes after his father," Finian goes on, the unspoken point being that Donal's father is a big man in County Clare, a managing director at the nuclear plant in Moneypoint. I'm actually surprised to know that Finian still cares about the good opinion of people back home. I'd thought he forgot about that when he cashed a cheque for $700 million.

"Do you think he's aware of where these force fields come from, at all?"

I turn my head in surprise, and suck in an involuntary gasp of pain. I'm still stiff from the beating Sam's thugs gave me.

"They're made by the wee aliens in there, according to Gordon."

I don't recall mentioning that to Gordon.

"They shit them out! Isn't that right, Gordon?" Finian chuckles. "The media'll go bananas. We've barely wrapped

our heads around the idea of growing petrol in the fields."
He's referring to biofuel, which still carries the stigma of the
pre-Railroad days when they used corn, not oilflowers from
Sirius Beta.

"One's always had the view that the Denebites drew no
lines between genetic engineering and other branches of
biotechnology," Gordon says deprecatingly.

He figured it out by himself, of course, damn him.

"They drew no bloody lines anywhere," Finian grunts.

"Quite. We still consider genetic engineering to be
somewhat immoral—a view I subscribe to myself—but the
Denebites had no such qualms. I believe these domes to be
…force field *factories.*"

Finian tilts his helmet at the massive dome rearing ahead
of us. "Is that smoke coming out of there?"

CHAPTER 15

The dumper truck swerves past us on its return journey to the airlock. Kenneth's jumping up and down in the skip on top of a load of snow. He, too, has seen the smoke emerging from vents high in the dome's sides.

It turns out that Denebite automation has forest fires covered.

The smoke from the burning trees streams upwards. There's a roaring noise of suction. An artificial gale blows, whipping the trees around, as fresh air is pumped into the dome at many times the normal rate.

I suppose this must have happened more than a few times in the dome's long history.

But I'm sure it's never before resulted from human interference.

Who knows how it happened? An accident, arson, an attempt to drive Donal and the others out of cover, a Care Bear cookfire carelessly scattered? Who cares?

It must have started near here. Some trees are black spars, others are untouched. The wind's pushing the flames away from us at a fast walking pace. A lurid red furnace glows through the trunks. I mooch along in my spacesuit, saying over the radio, "Donal! Harriet!"

Off to the left of me, Kenneth's shouting, "Vanessa! Honey! Baby! Please be alive!"

Finian and Gordon have gone in a different direction. They're probably searching for any surviving Care Bears of the Lost Planet.

That is what Finian was up to all along, of course, with his blather about how Donal is a 'good solid lad,' 'takes after his father'—he was trying to sound out my own loyalties, to see if I'd be open to cutting Donal out of the proceeds.

After all, that worked out so brilliantly for me the last time.

More generally, he'll have been trying to play me and Donal off against each other. That's been his game for ages.

Well, he'll be disappointed this time. I told him that I wasn't up for it, and anyway, Donal already knows about the Care Bears' hidden talents. He was with me at the historical moment when we became the first humans to witness A-tech biofactories pooping.

Force field bubbles bounce across the forest floor, carried on the wind. I kick listlessly at them, and change direction. I was heading for the lake, for want of any better ideas. But it's an inferno up that way. If Donal and the others hid there, they're already dead.

I am just wondering what happened to Sam Junior and his lads when chips fly out of a tree trunk in front of my face.

Oh Jesus! As if a forest fire wasn't enough to be dealing with!

I throw myself flat and crawl away from the flames. I

have my helmet on, to avoid the smoke, but now I can't stand being deaf, unable to hear which way the bullets are coming from. I pop my visor and inhale smoke-tinged air.

Wheeeee-BANG!

The bullets whistle as they tumble through the trees. Time to be elsewhere.

CRACK!

CRACK!

That's a different gun, firing supersonic rounds. I pop my head up—

—and one of those bloody maintenance robots nearly takes it off, striding over me.

The robot is dragging a hose.

I roll out of the way as several more maintenance robots pass by, carrying their sections of the hose.

Denebite Automation For Stopping Forest Fires, Part 2.

At close range, the robots launch a spray of water into the flames. I stumble the other way, thanking Jesus and Mary and all the saints.

My relief is shortlived.

I tumble down into a hollow I recognize; it was formerly full of mushberry vines. The Care Bears showed us how to harvest the berries by slicing through their stems with a sharp bit of bark.

Now it's full of charred debris, the fire already having passed through here, and force field bubbles, which are completely immune to fire of course. They fill the hollow, and thigh deep in them stands Finian, pointing his AR-15 at me.

That was the faster gun I heard.

"I thought you were Sam," he says, lowering his gun.

Then he reconsiders. "Well, you're in it with him, anyway." The AR comes back up.

He thinks *I* betrayed the expedition to Special Delivery Sam?!?

He's partly right, for it was someone on our crew, whose background we really should have checked out more thoroughly. But blaming Kenneth would not get me anywhere now. Finian has already made up his mind to shoot me, his own brother's son, for this imagined treachery.

I'm almost too gobsmacked to move.

Then I do, diving into the bubbles.

At the same time I hear the *wheeee-CRACK!* of the slower gun. That must be Sam, sniping at us from cover.

Finian yells a curse and drops the AR-15.

I scramble for it, burrowing through the bubbles, and my glove closes on the hot barrel just as Finian body-slams me. I rear back—my ribs screaming—and hurl the AR out of the hollow.

Finian lunges after it.

I stowed my lightsaber in my spacesuit's thigh pocket this time. I jerk my right glove off with my teeth and press the pushbutton. The bright blue beam leaps past Finian's shoulder, stopping him cold.

"Stand and face me if you're a real man!"

"Aw Jesus, you're not serious," Finian says.

"I am as serious as a fecking heart attack." I dial the beam down to the shortest setting. Now it's about the same length as a fencing foil. The scientists of Earth would give their collective left bollock to know how a beam of focused energy can be *short,* instead of carrying on to infinity the way energy's supposed to do.

"What is this, the classic movie channel?" Finian says.

"If you like." I nod at the little faces peeping over the rim of the hollow. "They lost their homes in a forest fire."

"You've got a smart mouth on you." Finian wrenches out his own lightsaber. "You're still crap in a fight."

His beam lances out, the same length as mine, the same bright blue—and that's when my own beam dies.

Out. Of. Charge.

Finian's rolling. He can hardly speak for laughing. "That never happened to Luke bloody Skywalker."

"Fletch!"

I jerk my head up. A small object comes flying end over end out of the charred undergrowth. I duck, and then see what it is, just in time to catch it in my left hand.

A spare powerpack.

"Thanks, Gordon." I slot it home.

"I believe in fighting fair," Gordon says, sat on a tree root, safely out of range.

"We'll discuss this later, Gordon," my uncle growls, and then he slashes at me, his beam sizzling through the debris drifting down from the burnt trees.

You can't parry with these things. Can't block, can't deflect the other man's beam with your own—they just go straight through each other. They're not really much like the ones in the films at all.

So Finian slashes at me, and I jump aside, which brings him lunging into the bottom of the hollow, and I swing my beam in a wide arc, not aiming at him, but at the thousands of force field bubbles stirred up around us.

They pop in their hundreds, shrivelling into silvery rags.

I keep on slashing.

A nasty rotten-egg smell wafts to my nostrils.

It is the smell of hydrogen sulfide gas.

Colorless, invisible, heavier than air, and highly toxic.

Finian is lower down in the hollow than me.

He looks puzzled.

Then he looks apoplectic.

Then he crashes onto his back, unconscious.

I slam down the visor of my helmet and drag him up out of the hollow by his heels, with help from Gordon. *Without* help from Gordon, I tie his wrists behind his back. It's a good thing I am an explorer who always carries string.

"He'll be spitting when he comes around," I say to Gordon. "Will you stay with him?"

"How did you know that would happen?"

"The first time we popped one, it smelled like a fart. I'd say the CBs' intestinal gases are far more toxic than ours, and that's why they evolved the forcefield bubbles, to keep the air in here from getting contaminated. It wasn't genetic engineering the Denebites did on them, so much as guided evolution."

"We'll make a stacker of you yet, Fletch."

"Feck off with your condescension."

I pick up Finian's AR-15. My ribs are really killing me now.

"Donal!" I shout, not very hopefully. "Donal, where are you?"

The fire's been beaten back from our immediate area. The trees are still whipping around, shedding burnt bits of leaf on us, like black rain. A dozen Care Bears of the Lost Planet, their fur caked with soot, huddle mournfully nearby.

"Donal!" I shout once more.

Someone answers me.

It is not Donal.

They aren't even speaking English.

Two fellas charge up to us, crashing through the burnt undergrowth, yelling in Russian.

I do not speak Russian, but it's pretty clear they're telling me to drop the AR-15. So I do.

They wear spacesuits that may have been white before they came in here. The faces in the open visors are narrow-lipped, fleshy and hard withal. They're mafiosi from Arcadia.

This might sound impossible to you—what the feck would mafiosi from Arcadia be doing here?—but there's no doubt about it, because the logos on their spacesuits say SAMSUNG.

CHAPTER 16

I've faced death before, and more often than not it has been Big Tech security contractors on the other end of whatever weapon was involved.

That I *am* facing death now, and not a nice trip back to Arcadia, seems certain.

Invaluable A-tech + Samsung security contractors + independent explorers on the scene first = dead independent explorers.

I know this is how they operate, you know it, the whole galaxy knows it, it's just that no one will call them on it because they're all holding tech stocks.

The equation looks even bleaker when we reach the airlock, and there's Donal, and Harriet, and Kenneth, and Vanessa, and Jasmine, all sat on the blackened grass, with two more mafiosi holding AK-47s on them.

We nod to each other—AKs pointing at your head tend to quell outpourings of joy and relief.

A few minutes later, more mafiosi plunge up with some new victims. The new lads are covered with soot, so it takes me a minute to recognize Sam. Half of his curly hair is gone.

His eyes glitter blue in his grimy face.

"How'd you escape the fire?" he says to Donal, who sneers and turns away from him.

"We took refuge in the lake," Harriet says. "The Care Bears were all doing it."

"And the treecats?"

Harriet manages a smile. "They're good swimmers, too."

"They ran off when we were captured," Vanessa says, shoulders slumped, jaw jutting, holding back tears. "Maybe they'll learn to get along with the Care Bears someday. When we're all dead and gone."

"Shut up," yell the Bratva—this is what they call themselves, the *Brotherhood,* believe it or not.

An hour or so passes. Finian—who's been out cold on the grass—groans. He opens his eyes, says, "Feck," and closes them again.

I sneak a glance at my wrist screen. One more hour until the truck goes out. It's like waiting for the bus, except we're waiting to die, and I can think of no way out of this, none at all.

Twenty minutes left to go. The Bratva order us to take off our spacesuits. This is it, then. Spacesuits are valuable. You don't want punters dying in them. It's these little efficiencies that make the stakeholders happy. Hail Mary, full of grace, the Lord is with thee. Blessed art thou amongst women, I don't want to die.

Finian, awakened with a kick, sees the same thing in his crystal ball as I do. He starts to argue for our lives. He speaks a bit of Russian, which makes the Bratva listen to him, but he has to lapse into English to make his points. These are:

- ◆ We haven't broken any laws (apart from wantonly murdering dozens of people, Finian, I think to myself)
- ◆ You can have the bloody A-tech
- ◆ You can have the ships, too
- ◆ Just give us a lift to Arcadia
- ◆ I'm famous, you know

To my surprise, this last point gains some traction. The boss of the security contractors, a fat lad who wears his watch *outside* his spacesuit for maximum bling value, says, "Ye-esss. You are Finian 'The Elephant' Connolly?"

"That's right, I am. Whatever you've heard about me, the truth is twice as bad." Finian grins in his filthy beard.

"He's a freaking legend," Sam pipes up. "He was gonna invade us, can you believe? My mom wanted the whole fleet obliterated, but when she heard it was Finian Connolly, she was like, well, actually, no. We can't kill *him*. Everyone in the business looks up to him. He's got a fan club."

Does Sam actually think this will help?

The boss of the subcontractors grins like a shark. "OK. We don't disappoint fan club. You, Mr. Connolly, we take back to nice comfortable jail cell. Rest of you, hurry up! Off those suits!"

"*Vot ty gde!*" sings out a new voice.

A Toyota Hummingbird comes zipping along the road that runs around the inside of the dome. The Hummingbird is a flitter, but it's not in the same class as the ones we used to carry on the *Skint Idjit*. This is more like a Prius with anti-grav. The tips of its stubby wings clip the burnt trees.

Hope surges when I see who's riding in the front passenger seat, next to the Bratva chauffeur.

Imogen!

I start up off my knees, shouting her name. One of our Bratva whacks me in the head with the stock of his AK. I sink down again.

The Hummingbird settles in front of the airlock. Imogen gets out, avoiding my eyes.

Oh *no*.

She used to work for the Bratva on Arcadia.

Correction: she never *stopped* working for the Bratva, obviously.

Why, why, why am I so gullible?

All she's ever wanted was to get her old tech job back. Now, apparently, she has. She's wearing a skin-tight spacesuit that must have cost a fortune, and across her lovely breasts it says SAMSUNG. She opens the rear door of the Hummingbird for an older fella wearing a slate-gray spacesuit, helmet off.

It's funny how you can always spot stackers, even when they're thousands of lightyears away from their green, ergonomic, organic offices. It's the glow of confidence. Gordon's got it, Milton's got it, even Ruby's got it, and this fella's got the world's supply of it. He smooths back his wind-ruffled silvery hair and flashes a laser-whitened smile at the security contractors. He must be at least a vice-president.

Finian starts to blether again, desperately. A boot in the kidneys shuts him up.

The vice-president affects not to notice. Maybe he really doesn't notice. Maybe he doesn't see us at all. He's chatting with the boss of the Bratva, and none of their talk is about the eleven people lined up on their knees, some out of their spacesuits, some half-disrobed. We've already ceased to exist.

"Imogen," I whisper. *"Imogen."*

Her eyes flick towards me, defiant, admitting no guilt.

"How'd you get in?"

"There are other airlocks, dummy. This dome is hundreds of kilometers in circumference. All the trucks go out at different times."

Oh.

She goes back to ignoring me, standing straight and respectful, waiting for the VP to need her. How could she do this to us? I remember our conversation beside the lake. She said that she felt relaxed here. That it was different and good. I'm *sure* she was speaking from the heart.

"They're going to kill us, Imogen."

"Don't be stupid," she hisses.

"As soon as your man's out of the way, it'll be curtains for us. You have to say something."

Nothing.

"It was them behind us on the Railroad, wasn't it? That ship blocking the Burren junction? That was a *Samsung* ship."

"TchVK Arcadia Security," she corrects me.

"How did they find us? I suppose they just followed Sam's lot?"

Imogen smiles faintly, and holds up a necklace she is wearing outside her spacesuit. It's one of those chunky ugly pendants she was selling on Arcadia. "Behold the Tangle."

"The what?"

"They come in pairs." She nods at the TchVK Arcadia Outsourcing boss's wristwatch.

"What are they?"

"Quantum-based FTL comms. A-tech, of course."

Jesus Christ, that's been on the top ten wish list forever. "Why haven't I heard about this?"

"No one else has, either," she whispers. "It's totally hush-hush. They haven't been reverse-engineered yet. There are only about twenty pairs in the universe."

And now we know about them, too, which gives TchVK Arcadia Security another reason to bump us off, if they needed one.

The VP is saying to the Bratva: " ... they'd be pretty cute if you cleaned them up. They look like Ewoks! Or is that just me? Anyway, I can totally see them as high-end pets."

Immersed in our own plight, I did not notice that the Bratva have caught some Care Bears of the Lost Planet. They now drag them closer for the VP's inspection. The poor things have leashes around their neck. They cringe, snivelling.

"Awww," says the VP, patting one on the head. Isn't it queer how he's warmed to them, whereas we, members of his own species, might as well not be here at all? He tells the Bratva, "Yeah, top priority is finding out where the force fields are manufactured. We might have to take the whole dome apart. But we'll definitely take some of these little guys home with us. Nice job, Sergei."

And it dawns on me.

They don't know where the force fields come from.

At the moment, myself, Donal, Gordon, and Finian are the only ones in the universe with that knowledge.

And very soon, Finian will be on his way back to Arcadia, possessing a secret worth billions—while our bones moulder on the Lost Planet ...

No!

Sheer rage jolts me to my feet. I'm talking loudly, before the Bratva can knock me down. "Sir! I know you've not had much time to observe them yet, but these little guys are actually intelligent."

The VP sees me for the first time. He raises his eyebrows.

"We've been here for weeks, living with them and communicating with them. They're talking to you right now! They're begging you to save them! They've been imprisoned here forever! It was the Denebites who victimized them and set up this horrible jail."

Kenneth figures out what I'm up to, and jumps in. "I'm a trained xenobiologist, and my observations support the conclusion that they are sophonts," he lies, desperately.

Gordon—who has been in the 'they're intelligent!' camp all along—concurs, in his educated stacker's tones. Finian scowls.

But the Samsung VP is not looking at either of them. He's looking from me to the Care Bears. The wheels of that well-polished mind are turning.

"They were trapped here, so they survived the fall of the Denebite Empire," I lay it out for him. "And here they are, and here you are, sir! In your position you can save them from further victimization!"

I stop there, wary of laying it on too thick.

But he's going for it. He is going for it! He's crouching, looking into the nearest Care Bear's eyes, and the little creature chooses this moment to growl in a way that sounds very much like talking. It stretches out its paw to touch the VP's face.

Maybe they *are* intelligent, at that.

Maybe they can tell that if there's one thing that gets a stacker even more excited than new A-tech, it is the prospect of being the first person to discover living, sapient aliens.

The VP stands up, trembling. "It's a distinct possibility," he says in a voice choked with emotion.

Finian blurts in rage, "They're never intelligent! They're just teddy bears that shit force fields!"

"They *what?*" shouts everyone who did not know this before.

"They produce force fields via their digestive processes," I say. I was going to play this card soon, anyway. "That is why the Denebites imprisoned them! Sir, it's as if aliens locked us up to harvest our skins or something! We must rescue them from their cruel captivity."

The VP nods decisively. "Regarding, um, shitting force fields, I'd have to see that to believe it. But are they intelligent? I'm gonna stick my neck out here and say ... Jesus, they *obviously* are!"

And with this I am content. He's heard what I have to say, and agreed with me. I exist for him now. Our lives are safe.

"What do you say, little guys?" the VP croons to the Care Bears. "We'll fix you up with a nice new planet, your sapient rights guaranteed, and in return you can, um—" he's giggling helplessly— "shit for us?"

He throws his head back, laughing, and I laugh with him, we all do (except Finian), chortling along as sycophantically as any Bratva.

We may not get any of the credit, and we won't get any of the money, but what does that matter? We'll get a lift back to Arcadia.

Which shows how little I understand the minds of Big Tech executives.

CHAPTER 17

"This," says Imogen, "fucking sucks." She flops down beside me. "I can't believe they left us here!"

We are sitting on the ground in the refugee camp the maintenance robots set up for the surviving Care Bears of the Lost Planet. Silver shacks, provided by the robots, gleam against the bleak burned forest. Baby Care Bears frolic around. Nearly all the forest is burned, and we're not allowed into the un-burned part. The robots are busy, taking cuttings and whatever else they're programmed to do, rejuvenating the forest. In the meantime we're living on tubers that taste like mashed potatoes without salt. We dig them up in the burned areas. They give everyone tummy-aches.

I continue flaking the charred shells off another basket of the horrible things, while Imogen vents her feelings.

"Three ships, *three*, and there wasn't room for us on any of them?"

The Samsung security contractors bumped us to make room for more Care Bears.

And adding insult to injury, Finian abandoned us, too. The minute the glow of TchVK Arcadia Outsourcing's thrusters faded in the sky, he took all three DC-100s and buggered off. Gordon went with him. They took the Old Elephants who'd been imprisoned on the *Bagged & Tagged,* our own South Africans, and a few of Sam Junior's surviving lads who were up for it. They've gone to bash Special Delivery Sam. That's why Finian came out this way in the first place, after all.

"You could have gone with them," I say to Imogen. "Nothing was stopping you. Finian said anyone could come if they were up for it."

"*Ucccch.* I am not the thrills and spills type." She gives me a wry glance. "I may have mentioned that before?"

I can see she's trying to coax a smile out of me, but she'll have to do more than be charming before I can forgive her. If not for her treachery, we'd be on our way back to Arcadia right now with a cargo hold full of Care Bears, and an obscenely huge payday awaiting.

Well, at least Finian didn't get the A-tech, either. So that's him paid back for cheating me out of my $280 million. It's cold comfort.

"There'll be no thrills where they were going," I say.

"Right? I am so not up for a buccaneering raid on Omega Centauri 49."

"He'll probably lose." I slide the basket of tubers towards Imogen. "Do you want to do some of these?"

As I suspected, she does not. She wanders off to seek sympathy elsewhere. I continue to clean the tubers. My hands are chapped, my nails torn, soot ingrained into the skin. My ancestors in the nineteenth century cleaned tatties with their hands, just like this, and they also suffered hunger pangs night and day.

But *they* did not have Hollywood deals, and video game

development deals, and their own line of perfumes.

What's that? you say. Ah, yes. Before the Samsung VP left, he got around to asking our names. When he heard Donal's name, he said that reminded him, the Goldman Sachs people on Arcadia had given him a letter for Donal if he should happen to meet us out this way.

The letter went: "Dear Mr. O'Leary, per section 144.6(b) of your contract, in lieu of your debt we have seized all rights to your poem *Feck Off With You: Butterfly-Zilla, An Epic Poem*. Your account is now closed. You should, however, expect no revenues relating to *Feck Off With You* or its related properties, including *Feck Off With You* (film), *Feck Off With You* (video game), the upcoming *Feck Off With You* clothing and fragrance line, or the *Feck Off With You* cooking school franchise and reality television show."

We were blindsided, as you would be. But the Samsung VP swore the letter was genuine, and then we remembered that before we left Arcadia, Donal put my poem on the internet. I'd said he could, not expecting anything to come of it. Now it turns out the bloody thing went viral. People want to hear about the trials we face in the exploration industry. So my poem's going to make millions ... for Goldman Sachs.

Congratulations, said the Samsung VP, and then he buggered off and left us.

We were quite elated, for about five minutes. Goldman Sachs won't be slapping liens on the houses of our families on Earth. That's something. It is not a small thing.

But we're still stuck on the Lost Planet, digging tatties up with sticks, and we're still broke.

The blasted tubers are not going to get any cleaner than

this, given the state of my hands. I carry them over to the cookfire and dump them into the pot.

Now it's time to go out and relieve Donal.

We're mending the *Intergalactic Bogtrotter*.

All the other players dismissed it as a wreck, and it is, it is. But you can do a lot with force fields.

We've got experience and motivation, and we've got a stacker: Ruby, who declined to go on the Special Delivery Sam-bashing expedition. He feels *very* betrayed by Finian. He wants to get back to Arcadia and start taking his meds again.

He will be disappointed, but he won't be the only one.

Shouldering my spacesuit, I set out on the long tramp to the airlock. I've got an hour before the truck, so I take my time. New green shoots haze the burnt forest floor. There's a tangy smell of fresh growth.

I'm surprised you didn't go with Finian, Donal said to me after my uncle left.

Why? I said.

Well, you nutted those two kids like it was nothing. I couldn't have done that. I never knew you had it in you.

I didn't know I had it in me either, I said with a laugh, and Donal looked at me as if I was a stranger.

I wanted to tell him then that I regret it every day. I slid one toe over the edge of the precipice, and I didn't like what I saw, so I pulled back. But I can't add to his trauma. He already feels guilty that I killed poor Annika and Jesse because he wouldn't or couldn't.

So I just said I didn't fancy Finian's chances, and that's why I didn't go with him. And this is perfectly true. I expect Finian will lose the battle and spend the rest of his days slaving for Special Delivery Sam in a rainy potato field. Or else the whole heap of them will be killed by Samsung's security contractors.

"What'll we do when they come back?" Donal said at the end of that conversation, his thoughts running along the same track as mine.

After congratulating us on clearing our debt to Goldman Sachs, the Samsung VP told us we'd better be gone when they come back for the rest of the Care Bears. This is their version of sparing our lives. We won't kill you *now*. We'll give you a couple of months to get clear.

We'll have the *Bogtrotter* spaceworthy in half that time.

But where'll we go in her? That is what Donal was asking, and when I said bleakly that I suppose we'd better go home, he got a fiery look in his eyes.

No, he said. No! We can't go home emptyhanded.

I never planned on it myself, Donal …

And we won't, he said. We'll turn this thing around. All we need is one little find.

One little find that isn't shite.

Trudging through the burnt forest towards the airlock, I preview his plan in my mind. It's so easy to visualize, it's as if it has already happened and I'm remembering it. We'll return along the Omega Centauri spur to the Burren. That's where we were attacked by Special Delivery Sam. They blew up three of Finian's ships but that leaves two, including the *Marauding Elephant*. They might have taken those two away (they certainly have, in my own opinion) but the wreckage of the others will be there. We'll forage for useful bits and parts, top up our water tanks, and then ho! for the Scutum-Centauri arm.

Donal's eyes were glowing and he picked up my hand and squeezed it for emphasis as he spoke, like an evangelist saving me from the fires of hell.

I wanted to get out of this life. When I think about all those unexplored planets on the Scutum-Centauri arm, it just makes me tired. But I couldn't say no to him.

Reaching the airlock, I sit down on my spacesuit and smoke a cigarette. I found a packet poor Jesse must have dropped. I've been eking them out, one a day.

"That's how the fire started," says a voice from the sky.

I nearly swallow my fag.

Sam Junior slides down the same big tree that me and Donal hid in during their raid. It's the first time I've seen him in a few days. Him and his friends, the ones that didn't join Finian, have been hanging out in a different part of the forest. When we have crossed paths there's been blaming and posturing.

No need for that when it's just him and me. I satisfy myself with a cold stare.

"Just make sure you put it out properly," he says.

His hair's growing back. He's covered with soot and scratches. They've not been eating any better than we have, by the looks of him.

"You're going out to work on your ship, aren't you?" he says.

"Yeah, we'll be leaving soon," I say. "We'll give you a lift to the Burren if you want."

"Screw the Burren. It's a nothing-burger." He sits down beside me. "We found your treecats."

"Did you?" Harriet and Vanessa will be overjoyed. "We were wondering where they went."

"They're in our camp. They're hella clever, huh?" He laughs.

"Are you thinking of taking them home to your mom?" I'm just twisting the knife. He hasn't got a ship to go home in.

"Screw my mom," he says, and the parts of his face that aren't soot-colored whiten with intensity. "I hope Finian kicks her ass into the Andromeda Galaxy."

"You should have gone with them."

"Fuck that. I'm sick of risking my life, for what? For bragging rights? Oh, I am the empress of a shitty fucking galactic cluster no one's ever heard of. Woo-hoo. No, no, man, I'm through with that."

"Congratulations."

He sighs. "If you and me had taken a bunch of force fields and gotten the hell out, no one would have ever been the wiser about this planet. It would have been our own private ATM, forever."

"I won't say that has not occurred to me." I drag on my cigarette and stub it out. The truck'll be here any minute. "But I don't believe in regrets. The best discovery is always the next one."

"Exactly. Exactly!"

"We're going to explore along the Scutum-Centauri arm," I tell him. "Out on the frontier. Lots of unexplored planets out there."

"The Scutum-Centauri arm?" he scoffs. "I've got a way better idea."

"Oh yeah?"

"Yeah. You've got a ship. I've got my mom's list of contacts. And we've still got the treecats."

"And?"

"Dude, didn't you ever notice? There is *nothing* they can't get into. They're the best thieves in the freaking universe ..."

Fletch's (mostly unwanted) adventures continue in the next volume of the *Interstellar Railroad* series, *Banjaxed Ceili.*

DISCOVER THE ADVENTUROUS WORLDS OF FELIX R. SAVAGE

An exuberant storyteller with a demented imagination, Felix R. Savage specializes in creating worlds so exciting, you'll never want to leave.

Join the Savage Stories newsletter to get notified of new releases and chances to win free books:

felixrsavage.com/signup

THE SOL SYSTEM RENEGADES SERIES

Near-Future Hard Science Fiction

A genocidal AI is devouring our solar system. Can a few brave men and women save humanity?

In the year 2288, humanity stands at a crossroads between space colonization and extinction. Packed with excitement, heartbreak, and unforgettable characters, the Sol System Renegades series tells a sweeping tale of struggle and deliverance.

Crapkiller
The Galapagos Incident
The Vesta Conspiracy
The Mercury Rebellion
The Luna Deception
The Phobos Maneuver
The Mars Shock
The Callisto Gambit

Keep Off The Grass (short story)
A Very Merry Zero-Gravity Christmas (short story)

THE RELUCTANT ADVENTURES
OF
FLETCHER CONNOLLY
ON THE
INTERSTELLAR RAILROAD

Near-Future Non-Hard Science Fiction

An Irishman in space. Untold hoards of alien technological relics waiting to be discovered. What could possibly go wrong?

Skint Idjit
Intergalactic Bogtrotter
Banjaxed Ceili
Supermassive Blackguard

FIRST CONTACT, INC.

Not A User's Manual

The alien rulers of the galaxy are pyramid marketers, and humanity's role in the grand scam is to play the sucker at the bottom.

Unless we can find suckers of our own to prey on ...

Against The Rules

Payback